The Faithful Enemy

The Faithful Enemy

Varun H. Parmar

PARTRIDGE
A Penguin Random House Company

ISBN: Softcover   978-1-4828-6943-9
             eBook   978-1-4828-6942-2

To order additional copies of this book, contact
Partridge India
000 800 10062 62
orders.india@partridgepublishing.com

www.partridgepublishing.com/india

Contents

Acknowledgements.

Firstly, I would like to thank Lord Swaminarayan and my guru His Divine Holiness Pramukh Swami Maharaj without whose mercy and grace I wouldn't be able to compile this book.

Then I thank the BAPS Children's Forum with the help of whom I obtained creative ideas and got the inspiration to write.

I then thank my childhood teacher Mrs. Ida D'mello with whose guidance I have been able to write and express myself as clearly as possible.

I would also like to thank my parents for shaping up my life and making me rise to become something special on this earth. They constantly motivated me to complete my book. I'm grateful to them.

I would also like to thank my friends Dhruv Kedia and Shreyas Krishnan who were among the first ones to encourage me to write and complete my book.

I would then like to thank Kervi Udani, who constantly asked me about the book and expressing her innermost desire to read it.

I would like to thank my friends Mohit, Rajeev and Bhavin, who have been my readers and have constantly urged me to write more and more.

I express my thanks to Harsh Patel and Geet Kalda, who despite knowing little about the book, constantly kept me busy in completing my book.

The next ones in the list I want to thank are Nidhi Ingole, Himani Sarda, Kush Shah, Vivek Shah, Yashica Bharvesh and Radhika Bagri, who constantly kept themselves updated with the news of my book and in turn keeping me aware that I had a book to complete.

Next I would like to thank Simran Makhija, Yash and Asmita, who also kept me aware that I had a book to complete and constantly encouraging me for it.

I want to thank Aayushi Dave, Manav Jain, Usman Dhange, Samrudhi Chandekar, and Madiha Shaikh who have constantly encouraged me to write and complete the book, and have also made significant contributions in the book making, since the time they met me.

I thank Bill Gates and all the software designers who have made it possible for me to express myself in the Microsoft Software.

Thanks to Yanessa Evans, the senior publishing officer of the Partridge Publishing Company and Pohar Baruah, my Publishing Services Associate, who constantly kept a follow up of what I was doing and helped my book get published.

In the end, I would like to thank Partridge Publishing Company without whose help; I would not have risen to become an author.

Chapter 1

The Eight Amigos

19th January 2012
Dublin

The eight friends met again at Malcolm's house. They had to discuss about what to cook at the school's cooking competition. After a long silence Mark burst up.

'Is anyone going to suggest anything?'

'Pizzas. I am an expert in making them,' said Malcolm.

'Burgers are the easiest to make. Just cheese, potatoes, cabbage, icebergs and tomatoes. Spread some mayonnaise on the top and the bottom side. Pile the ingredients one above the other and you're done,' Ian said.

'Why not Chinese noodles with some fried rice and some Manchurians on the top of that with some soup and a bar of chocolate.........

'Where on Earth do you find a bar of chocolate with Chinese food, huh Louis?' asked Malcolm

'Why not? You can use that bar of chocolate as a sweet dish after the food,' and he let out a cold laugh.

'Changing this guy needs a lot of patience,' Ian muttered under his breath.

'And by the way, this is not a restaurant competition Louis. It is a food cooking competition,' Fred grumbled.

'Think of something different. Think critically guys.' Katie said.

'Pasta?!' said an excited Kathy.

'Nah. I think of crispy sandwich pizzas,' Emma said. All eyes turned towards her. It was a definitely different idea. 'Make bread kind of stiff by toasting them and then cut them into two. Garnish the thing with some sauce, tomatoes and an ample of cheese. Our stuff is ready.'

Everyone gaped at her, lost in thought. They appreciated her suggestion very much and set out to work right from the next day. They aimed for success in their item for the next seven days. For the first time when they tried making the thing out it was over toasted and what they got was just a mass of coal. They got it right at the third time and they got so overwhelmed on their success that they had a real feast on it. They tried out their luck in school. And guess what? Their group bagged the first position. ? They danced in ecstasy.

These eight friends called themselves 'The Eight Amigos'. All had the same passions and the same thoughts and were equally distributed with the power of knowledge. All were born with a very powerful brain. Always gained the top positions in everything, may it be studies or external exams.

Mark was a good natured fellow but with a summery mind. He liked computers very much and was all into technology. He spent a great deal with computers and helped his group in all computer related projects. He was a dashing fellow with smart looks and shiny black hair.

To talk for Louis, he was a great fan of food. A hefty fellow interested in robotics other than food. He had a habit of taking examples of food while talking about anything. But he still was a lot helpful for science projects they got in school.

Ian was an intelligent guy, smart and brainy. He experimented much and away from rest of the world, he loved cycling a lot. When he would participate in the school cycling race, the cup would already be made with his name inscribed on it. But he was exceptionally good in studies as well.

Malcolm, a great gentleman personality right from his childhood would always try taking great risks. But he was much more interested in becoming a businessman, one of the world's greatest. A peaceful man with a smile always on his smart face.

Fred too was a risk taking man and always accompanied Malcolm. Both were the best of friends. He was but a person who always remained confused in really critical situations. His smart mind but won the hearts of everyone. His passion of swimming fetched him the first prize at the swimming competition every year. He aimed at becoming the world champion at the Olympics.

Kathy, a live and a very active girl was very studious. She had taken part in many competitive exams and bagged the first prize in many of them. Mathematics was her specialty. A firm follower of the Indian mathematician Ramanujan.

Emma was one of the most 'different thinkers' of their group. The suggestions given by her were always effective and correct. She too, like Kathy was interested in mathematics and science. She aimed at becoming a scientist. Her inspiration was the great Marie Curie. Her passion included only and only studies.

Katie was a philosopher, providing knowledge to all around her. She was a blonde haired cute girl but when angered, there would be o one to pacify her.

This group was a really inseparable group. They helped each other in times of difficulties and supported each other in times of happiness. They were actually made for each other. Their friendship was praised all within their city. It was a bond of close friendship, a bond of love between them. No one knew what great things were due to be done by them. The Eight Amigos.

Chapter 2

The Great Meet

The Eight Amigos met each other after six long years of hard work and studies. After each one of them got a graduation degree in hand, they all decided to meet each other after a gap of such a long time. The place to meet was decided as fast as lightning. 'The Indian Sultanate'. A gorgeous hotel which was best known for its service in the traditional Indian way. The upper part of the walls was cream colored, lighted with yellow lights marking the olden Indian times of Kings and the Maharajas. The lower parts of the walls were carved out of wood marking the great Indian handicrafts. A great hall within the hotel, better known as the' Courtroom' of the hotel was in its full grandeur. In the midst of all this sat the eight friends, enjoying each others' company after six long years.

'Guys, tell you what? I'm an M.Sc in Chem. now!' Ian said. 'Really enjoyed all these years studying but alone without you all. Fred was with me. He's done the ……

'M.Sc in Physics and Chem.,' Fred said, interrupting Ian.

'I've finished my course in photography and philosophy,' Katie said proudly.

'Is that a thing to boast about?' Fred whispered in Ian's ears and both went in a fit. Katie glanced a fiery look at them. They stopped laughing. 'I mean where does that match, photography and philosophy?'

'None of your business,' Katie said and resumed fidgeting on her phone.

'And I'm a ……Kathy said but was interrupted by Fred.

'M.Sc in Mathematics. Correct?'

'Precisely,' Kathy said. 'And a master mathematician.' She said with a beaming smile on her face.

'Robotics engineer here,' Louis said, raising his hand.

'Any guesses about me?' Malcolm asked, grinning. Everyone' s mouth hanged. Had Malcolm spoken? They thought.

'Yup, an automobile engineer,' said Louis and burst out in laughter.

'No teasing me with science Louis. You now I loathe it. I am a businessman already,' Malcolm said with a sly grin again.

'Already,' all said at the same time getting up from their chairs. It was a real shock for them. He had proceeded onto his field while they were still there with degree in hands.

'Yeah, I am a year older than you guys, remember?'

'Oh yes,' all relaxed into their chairs again.

'Okay, so? Is everyone done?' asked Ian. Sipping his orange-pineapple juice.

Juice? Yes, juice. These eight believed in diet and health too much. Never accepted anything out of their diet. The most firm of all was Katie. Suddenly she burst out,

'Emma's not here yet.'

'Oh, she? She's gone to India to pursue her higher studies,' Katie said. 'It's always a good hub for education, India, isn't it?'

'Yes, always. I have a great passion of being in India. I want to be in India at least once for sure. It is the mother of us all. I feel like I'm an Indian when I talk about India,' Malcolm said and he saw what he thought would be said next.

'Yes, yes. Right Mark. Now listen guys. I want you tell you something. Something cryptic. Something strong. Something great,' Ian said with grimness suddenly spread all over his face.

'What is it Ian?' Fred asked, leaning a bit towards Ian.

'Have you guys, especially Malcolm, wondered what is the condition in India. The people of India are dying of hunger. The old ruling party's political leaders have consumed all the money needed for the upliftment of India. We have to help the new government in some way. Any way that can bring back the pride of India. That can make India a better country again.'

'Actually we're not Indians. Why worry about India?' Kathy asked.

'India is the motherland of this whole world. We should worry about India. I'll explain everything later. Firstly, you all ready to help?' Ian asked. Everyone looked at each other' s faces not knowing what to do.

'Explain the matter at least Ian,' Katie said.

'Okay. In the Indian state of Gujarat, between the hills of the very famous mountain range called Girnar, fifth hill from the north and the second in it, there lies something which Indian people do not know yet, except the old government of course. It is what was India's. It is what only India used to mine in the olden times. It is for what Indians would dearly fall. It is something worth a lifetime.'

'Come directly onto the point, Ian,' Louis said grumbling.

'Okay. I want you all to know about the gold which is hidden among the the great Indian State of Gujarat.'

'What?' everyone gasped at the same time. The people from the tables around them were interrupted by this loud noise and turned all their eyes towards the group. Malcolm suddenly stood up and said

'Sorry fellas, extremely sorry. You may carry on now. We won't disturb again,' he said with forty parts of anxiousness and sixty parts of apology. All resumed their works with a look of disgust.

'Phew! That was close,' Ian said, letting out a wisp of air. 'Anyway, what I'm saying is absolutely true. It is going to be auctioned surprisingly by the old government on 6th February 2020. What's today's date, huh Katie?'

'Umm,' she said, checking out her watch, 'Today is 6th November 2019, Ian.'

'Exactly three months from now. I am going on that mission. Of sneaking the gold out and helping the Indian poor as far as I can. I need help,' Ian said disappointedly.

Everyone was awestruck. Ian was mad. Helping the Indians, sneaking thegold out of the mountain ranges. It all seemed utterly nonsense to them.

'I know it seems rubbish to you, but the old government has the gold in its hand as well as the money which they have looted from the common people. I'm very concerned about them. Please help me,' Ian said.

After a great deal of silence, Jeremy spoke out, 'You're mad Ian.'

'Not an issue,' Ian said.

'For what?'

'Not helping me.'

'Who says no one is helping you?'

'You did.'

'When did I say that? Of course we can't step back when one of our friend is embarking upon the greatest danger of his life. Can we guys?'

'No,' came the reply from all of them.

'You see Ian, we' re your best buddies. I mean anything for our amigo, right? Cheer up now,' Jeremy said. Ian smiled. All smiled in joy.

'So, where do we start?' asked Kathy, suddenly reducing the festive din of the amigos.

'We start at that place where the Indians might be able to get to know about their heritage,' Ian said.

'What do you mean?' asked Katie.

'We start by returning their own things to them. Their pride and honor.'

'But what is that?' asked Jeremy.

'You sure about doing this? I mean executing this type of robbery?' Malcolm asked worried.

'No,' was Ian's reply. Just a calm no.

'We need plans,' said Katie.

'I have them all ready.'

'We need tools,' said Kathy.

'I have all contacts ready.'

'Then what are we waiting for?' asked Mark.

'To pounce upon the Kohinoor.'

Chapter 3

London

'Actually, we need to prepare ourselves for this great and risky, although thrilling adventure. Shouldn't we, Ian? Asked Kathy.

'Unbelievably, yes,' he replied.

'We need a lot of things before we execute it. Ammunition, protective garments, communication media, and yes, the most important of all, carry your smart-watches. I'll update the latest softwares in it,' Louis said.

'We don't need to worry about the ammunition and the other stuff. I've ordered it already. Antony will be here by 7pm. Mark, go to Beamland Hotel, Room no. "719" and bring all the stuff. Got it? Good. And for Louis point of the smart-watch, it is an absolutely essential thing in our mission. Don't forget to carry it. Forgot your clothes? Doesn't matter. Forgot your SW, there is a big matter and only matter,' Ian said.

'SW? a puzzled Malcolm asked.

'Smart-watch,' Fred said with a snap, smiling.

'Oh. Clear your meanings Ian.'

'I will,' Ian said.

All of them had their bags packed and were sitting for the right time to come, for going to the airport of course. Their flight was due at 10:30pm. Mark had gone to bring the stuff. He would directly meet all of them at the airport. At 7pm exact, the punctual seven left their Berlin homes. This was the first step towards endangerment of their lives. No one cared about it. Relieving the mankind of its bad state had become their goal. They reached the airport.

'They seven guys put themselves forth into their own private plane. They had bought it in a partnership. Children of multi-millionaires you see. The plane was exactly like a private one, but a dashing streamlined design, and amazing features. For the cockpit, it was just a piece of glass with microprojectors fit inside it. Four options suddenly flashed on it. The Control Panel, Meters, Location and Temperature, and Miscellaneous. For additional features, the plane was governed by the SW. A smart-plane, with two smart TVs on side, sofas and much more than a private plane. A large plane but a private one. The plane took off, piloted by Louis. When it reached an altitude, Louis put the plane on the automatic mode and went out of the cockpit to enjoy with his friends. It wasn't a too long distance, but the seven enjoyed well.

The soaring plane soon arrived out of the cool mild clouds and into the grey atmosphere of London. The great sight of the city left them awestruck every time they visited this place. The mighty Thames enjoying jumping up and down, the Tower bridge resting on top of the river, The houses of Parliament showing its decorum, the Buckingham Palace showing its grandeur, the Tate Modern, the National museum, Madame Tussad's museum and much more. They went on to land on the London city airport. They drove their hired cars near the University of London, where they had hired a house. They moved in with all their bag packs and took a room each.

It was a beautiful house which they had rented. The milk white interiors and the dashing maroon carpet were really amazing. It was well furnished with the top quality wood available in England. The sofa sets and the tables around were really very amazing. There great chandelier that hung above their heads enhanced the beauty of the house more. There was a great big portrait of a man, young and healthy in his thirties. He looked somewhat like their gone-to-India friend Emma. All of them were well contented with the house. It was very much suitable for carrying out their activities.

They all met at 4 pm in the main hall. The white sofas added the beauty of the hall on which they sat. Louis started then, his mouth full of cheese balls, 'So, guys. Where is it?'

'Where is what?' asked Fred.

'That,' Louis said again.

'That what? Fatty!' said Fred again a little annoyed.

'He's talking about the diamond dumbos,' Ian said. 'Anyone has any idea where is it?'

All fell silent. Only the munching of Louis's cheese balls was heard. After a great deal of silence, Malcolm spoke up.

'I know. I know where it is.'

'Where?' all asked in unison.

'On the very top floor of the eastern sided tower of the one of the greatest and most fabulous bridges in the world. The Tower Bridge.'

'Are you sure? I mean is it really there?' said an awestruck Mark.

'Yup.'

'What plans do we have then to bring it within our arms? Anything prepared yet, Ian? Asked the curious Mark.

'We'll go there and act directly,' said Ian with a calm note.

'He's gone nuts. I … I mean we have not prepared anything and we go there without having seen the place and act directly, huh?' said an irritated Fred.

'More about that later……'

'He's gone mad!' Fred whispered to Louis while Ian was speaking.

'First the outlines about the place where the Kohinoor is,' Ian said. 'If you can please, Malcolm, show the info about that place.'

'Sure I will, Ian,' said Malcolm and after fidgeting on his SW projected the thing on the wall in front of them. It read as follows.

Tower Bridge

Built in ancient times, this famous bascule bridge contains many of the world's famous historical artifacts. One of them is the Kohinoor, a diamond brought by the British from India. It is a rare and a very expensive diamond. If a mountain of money was given in return of the diamond, it would amount to a very less price for it. Such is its rarity.

The museum at the top of each tower contains a special security system. A very delicate and a very powerful one. If even a thing as light as a pin falls on the ground, it is nearly impossible for anyone to escape, because an alarm rings as soon as the thing comes in contact with the ground and in just 240 seconds the whole place is surrounded by the police....

'Which means, 4 minutes,' said Katie instantly.

'That's fast calculation, huh?' Ian said smiling.

...provided the museum is closed for the day or a holiday. The eastern tower contains a number of secret passages. The most common of them being 'Passage 4'. There is no chance of anyone even thinking to enter theses towers.......

'It is really pretty hard to go through our plan,' Kathy said.

'Okay guys, listen to my plan....' but Ian was interrupted by Louis.

'You said we didn't have any plans, didn't you Ian?' said Malcolm, raising his brow, with an interrogated look.

'I was just kidding buddy,' Ian said. 'Now listen.........'

The morning of the planned day dawned. All were up early and travelled 20 miles from their place to examine the jet they had ordered. Black to camouflage the night sky, with high quality things inside. Sofas, tables and everything. Could be controlled by the SWs. It had bright white lights on its bottom. The seven friends were contented with it. It was going to be the most riskiest and dangerous day in their whole life, but they overcame their fear and put forth their first foot to face the fears and dangers of life.

Chapter 4

The Great Escape

It was 12 am. The streets of London were quiet and misty. The sky had blackened. It was cold and silent all around. The whole London save the police was in deep sleep, fatigued from the day's work. The tower bridge's two parts had been up again.

And suddenly, there came a booming voice. It was of a jet plane, black in color and with a high speed. It passed over the Eastern Tower of the Tower Bridge, and vanished quickly. There was no one to see it, notice it.

After about half an hour, an alarm started ringing. The police had rushed onto the spot from where the voice was coming. It was a loud alarm. People woke up. Thieves took up the advantage of pick pocketing people. Others came onto the window of their houses. No one had expected such a thing in the history of their lives. An alarm ringing at the Tower Bridge! Yes, the Tower Bridge. Surely there was something wrong inside there.

After a few minutes, a man was seen coming out of the broken window of the Eastern Tower of the Bridge. He was fully dressed in black. And then there came a jet plane with bright white lights. A man stood on the door of the plane and was murmuring something to the man on the Tower. The man in the plane suddenly stretched out his hand. The man on the tower jumped and caught his hand but suddenly lost grip and fell. But he opened up a parachute and smoothly came down.

And as he landed, the police force surrounded him from all sides. They all loaded their guns at once and there were about 25 guns pointing towards the man. The man remained as calm as ice. One of the policemen, who seemed to be the leader, came forward, his gun still pointing towards the man.

'Hands up.'

'As you say,' said the man and raised his hands.

'Who are you?'

'No one.'

'We all saw you jumping from the tower. Is this true?'

'My, my. Are you TV news reporter,' the man said and grinned. 'And on top of everything you saw me jumping and still you're asking. That was utterly ridiculous.'

'Confess your crime,' said the policeman.

'Well, why not. Do you know India?'

'Yes, why wouldn't I?'

'Good. That was the reason.'

'That really did not make any sense, man.'

'It will soon,' said the man and all of a sudden the black jet came with a very high speed. It descended gradually and passed over the police leader and the man. The whole police force ducked for their lives and the next second they saw the man had disappeared.

'Where is he?' the leader policeman shouted at the top of his voice. 'Rush upstairs to the tower. See what is missing. GO!' he bellowed.

At once, five policemen rushed up. After about 20-30 minutes, one of the policemen shouted from above.

'Sir, nothing has been stolen.'

'Good Lord! Come down now,' the leader policeman said.

'But except the …'

'Except the what?'

Except the …'

'Except the what? I can't hear you.'

'The Kohinoor.'

'You have got too much bravery, huh Ian?' said Malcolm to the hanging Ian below the jet.

'Shut up Malcolm. The helicopter there's following us. That black colored one,' Ian shouted.

'Close the door Malcolm. The plane is being imbalanced,' said the pilot Louis.

'Okay,' and Malcolm closed the door of the jet.

They were above the Thames River.

Ian stuck to the plane with his full body magnetic suit and observed the helicopter closely. It actually was police helicopter and was actually chasing them. As soon as Ian took out his gun, the helicopter started swaying in the air. Who knew that Ian was a gold medalist in the national shooting games? He had even hit a bull's eye when the target was in motion.

Shot one. The bullet hit the helicopter body and a small spark was produced.

Shot two. It hit the helicopter's front part. The helicopter started swaying more badly than it was.

Shot three. It was aimed for the pilot's head. It broke the glass instead.

Shot four. Aimed for the pilot but the bullet went off into the air. The grey cold and misty air.

Ian now had just two shots left. Just two bullets between the game of life and death. Just two bullets between the freedom and captivity. Just two bullets between him and India.

Shot five. He pulled the trigger with firm determination this time. The bullet missed the head just by an inch.

This was the last bullet and the last shot he had. This was his life decision. As the thinking process was going on, he felt the sudden weight of gravitation and he lost his balance. His legs lost the magnetic effect and hanged. At the same time Ian swayed a little and suddenly pulled the trigger in order to grip which he caught. The very 2nd second the bullet hit the man and there was blast, fiery and loud. Ian's hair swished back. Malcolm suddenly opened the door of the plane.

'Pull me up Malcolm,' Ian shouted, hanging uncontrollably.

'Mark, pass me the rope.' And the next five minutes saw Ian aboard.

'Welcome aboard,' said Katie.

After he had relaxed, he put aside his glass of water and lay down on the bed heavily. Ian was too tired to speak up.

All the others gathered around his bed. The jet was on the auto-pilot mode.

'Hey, you did a great job huh Ian?' said Louis.

Ian nodded, eyes still closed.

'You escaped narrowly, just because of that fatty,' said Mark and burst out laughing.

Ian nodded again, eyes still closed. It was their legacy, he thought. His first part of the dream came true.

'Let him get some sleep guys,' Katie said, going back to the sofa on which she sat.

And Ian slumbered into deep sleep.

'Hey! Hi!' said Mark as Ian opened his eyes. He wasn't aware of anything that happened.

'Where are we?' he asked subconsciously, rubbing his eyes.

'At Kathy's building of course,' said Katie, smiling at his subconscious state of mind.

And he focused. Yes, they were in Kathy's seven storeys building in Berlin. In front of him he could clearly the seethe big colossal portrait of the Indian scientist S.Ramanujan. Accompanying him was the great mathematician G.H.Hardy. To make sure still, he whistled once and the lights turned off and the television started. Then he half-whistled and the lights were on again. Now he was contented. It was Kathy's building or her home.

'Now Ian,' said Fred, 'you got to tell us about what happened there inside.'

'He's right,' all of them said in chorus and then started looking at each other. What a coincidence!

'Wait but…….' But Malcolm stopped Ian. 'No buts and ifs.' And then all started insisting him to tell about what had happened. Suddenly Louis caught something been said on the TV.

'Shhhh! Everyone, please calm down. Look there,' and he pointed towards the TV. 'And listen too.'

'Lame Louis, very lame,' said Kathy and looked towards the TV.

'The Kohinoor, the most amazing and precious diamond of all times has been stolen this morning at around 12:30 am. The police are still in search of it. It was extremely impossible to execute it. But it was still stolen,' the newswoman said.

'You've made the headlines Ian,' said Mark clapping on his back.

'That's not a thing to get ecstatic about, my dear friend,' said Ian, still very drowsy.

'The London police reported that it saw the jet which helped the thief getting away. They made sure they followed them but.....'

'That was the police helicopter you destroyed Ian,' Louis said loudly.

'Shut up fatty acid,' said Fred annoyingly while still gazing at the news lines. Louis grunted.

'The London police also reported that they had seen the man right in front of them but did not manage to capture him. "He escaped in front of our eyes while we ducked to save ourselves from that life seizing jet" a policeman said. Here's a picture as to how the man looked like,' and as the newswoman said that, a picture taken by someone of Ian standing between the pack of hungry wolf—policemen flashed.

'That is going to viral on the net,' Mark said.

'That was a very daring feat,' Katie said while switching off the TV.

'Of course it was,' said Mark, thumping himself on the bed. 'What do we have on our list next?'

'Huh?' said Malcolm, making a weird face, with a crooked expression.

'He's right Malcolm. We've got to advance onto our next step. As soon as possible,' Ian said.

'But we've just come out of this danger. We don't want another one right on heads and that too, just after this,' Malcolm said, a bit worried.

'We have to proceed, my friend, keeping the Indians in mind,' Ian said.

'But don't you think we're gonna go a bit fast, Ian?' Katie asked sweetly.

'Yes we are,' said Ian, falling back on the bed. 'But determination is leading me into starting a new adventure again.'

'We already have one waiting,' Fred said.

'Yeah! Other than this one, right?,' and Kathy laughed, taunting Fred.

'Actually Kathy is right.'

Everyone's eyes widened. Fred got up and started walking all around the room.

'Other than this new adventure we are going to start, there already lies a mystery ahead us to be solved,' he said gravely.

'Don't speak so seriously Fred. You're freaking me out. I'm sure it's not connected to underworld ghosts,' Louis said, perspiring. Louis was very much afraid of ghosts. If you talked about one, he would regain consciousness after about three hours.

'It's something connected with the underwater unidentified things,' he said.

'What are you exactly saying?' Ian got up and said.

'All about that later. Don't divert your minds. Now tell us Ian, what to do next?'

'Next is something again connected to India,' Mark said, foolishly.

'We know that, you fool,' Kathy said, and both the girls started giggling.

'You'll pay for that,' Mark said under his breath.

'We're now going to go for such a thing, never even dared to be touched,' Fred said.

'What is it?' asked Kathy curiously.

'It is the slit of immortality....'

'A knife,' Louis sprung up. Everyone looked at him with narrowed eyes. 'I'm sorry,' he said and sat down.

'So, it is the thing with the slit of immortality and the handle of victory. The sword of Tipu Sultan,' Fred said pumping out his chest and standing in a king's posture.

'Which Sultan?' said Katie, sure about having heard about that person for the first time.

'Tipu Sultan,' Fred said. 'The king of the Mysore state in India. One of the greatest kings ever. Could challenge the British exceptionally well. The inventor of rockets, which were very first used in his wars.'

'You mean, back to London again?' said a bewildered Ian, ruffling his hair.

'Actually yes,' said Fred.

'Will anyone tell us what is going on here? We can't understand a bit of all what you're talking,' Malcolm said, little annoyed.

'The sword of Tipu Sultan lies in London. We have to go there again,' Ian said.

'Where exactly in London?' Katie asked puzzled.

'The Tate Modern.'

'You mean the place beside the Thames?' shouted Louis.

'Be a little low Louis. Yes, the place, rather the museum beside the Thames,' said Fred.

'Off to London then, again,' said Kathy.

'For what?' asked Mark.

'To see the place of course. None of us has been there,' said Katie getting up.

'We even hadn't seen the Kohinoor, still we did it,' Mark said, his brows up, tensed.

'But we need to go for this and it is final. Got it Mark?' Ian said strictly.

'Yes,' Mark said.

'Good. So when do we leave for London again?' asked Fred.

'Two days would do,' Ian said.

'Then we have today and the next 48 hours still left to leave,' said Malcolm.

'Oh my cryptic friend Malcolm, come on the point,' said Louis.

'The time now all yours Ian,' Malcolm grinned.

Chapter 5

The Riddle

'As the plane of ours passed over the Eastern Tower of the Tower Bridge, I jumped down, fortunately on the desired spot, just a little lower. I was then on the sloping roof surface of the tower. I was losing balance but held grip somehow. Slowly and steadily I climbed up to the window's level. I was scared, seeing the height at which I was.'

'The from my parachute cum backpack I took out the chisel and the hammer. I looked here and there to see if there was no one. I was safe. I carefully placed my chisel on the top right corner of the window. It broke gently and softly. I removed the pane slowly and thrust it into the Thames.'

'When I looked back inside the window, there were a great lot of things there. The Kohinoor would be, I thought, well concealed. I activated my magnetic suit and jumped directly onto the metal ceiling of the museum, with my heart in my mouth.'

'I felt like Spider-Man at that time. Hanging up there was great but slow. I crawled all around the place up there like a lizard. I saw many things. Ancient Egyptian artifacts and Indian artifacts. Things from Greece and Rome. A small model of the Pantheon and other Greek buildings also adored the place. I was helped by the faint light coming in through the window in addition with the light of my smartwatch.'

'And the n suddenly my legs lost balance. They started groaning in pain because of the gravity. And they detached themselves from the ceiling. Down they came, and there I was, hanging on the ceiling with the support of just my hands. My legs were about just an inch from the ground. I was saved. I tried to stick myself up the ceiling wholly, but the gift of Newton wouldn't let me. I tried once, twice, thrice but no avail.'

'I lost about seven minutes in that process. I was about to give up when I thrust myself upwards. Forgetting the pain of my person, I did what I needed to. I thrust myself upwards with a great force. And I did impale on the metal canopy.'

'I balanced for about a minute and then resumed my quest for the diamond. I crawled and crawled. And before I could have the time to think to realize and save myself from the cornered wall, I butted in it.'

'And that was the co incidence. My smartwatch's light turned to the object I was below. And there was a sudden blazing shine. A very bright glow indeed. I looked down and faced the watch up. And I saw the lingering light of my smartwatch in the shine of the Kohinoor.'

'I was so much delighted. I could not hide my happiness. I had reached there with so much ease, rather difficulty. I wished to scream but you guys well knew the consequences. One scream and a force of merciless policemen, staring and pointing their guns right at you. I controlled myself.'

'I thought to pick up the diamond as fast as I could and then leave from there but I had to manage the body weight as well. With very much care of not losing the magnetic attraction with the metal roof, I spread forward my hands to grab the diamond.'

'And when I touched it, it was a purely normal feeling to touch but a great victory had taken place in the heart and the mind. It was screaming to get out of the body and into the world. I really lost control of my feelings.'

'It was then that I suddenly realized that I had to pack up as fast as possible and return to you guys. With trembling hands and an exhilarating feeling, I picked up the diamond and somehow managed to put it in the backpack. And then I started my way back to the window.'

'I switched off the smartwatch light and proceeded with the help of the faint light penetrating through the window. It was pitching black there inside.'

'I didn't have much to fear about my body for I had an armor on my body, metal plated and quite a few guns with me. I did have many gadgets along with me. And that's what when the great event took place.'

'I eventually had some bullets on my wrist in the form of a bullet wristband. Accidentally, one of the bullets fell on the hypersensitive floor. The alarm started ringing immediately. Good that I was near the window I had broken. I got down and got out of the window. I started the stopwatch, timing four minutes.'

'Getting out of the window and doing all that stuff took about twenty seconds…..'

'You calculated that too mad man?' interrupted Louis suddenly. Everyone gave some fierce looks at him. 'Sorry,' he had to say at last.

'No problem Louis. I'm just guessing. And now I had just few seconds around 200 left. I climbed the slope of the tower as fast and as high could. I was already out of energy. That hanging upside down thing took too much energy. And then I was where you saw me standing.'

'After about a few seconds I heard gloomy voice below me, within the museum. "Hands up, hands up" it said and it was true as I heard the clicking voice of the guns' loading too. I was terrified. How could I commit such a grave mistake I thought.'

'I held my breath. The men in the museum chamber were holding one of the most dangerous weapons in the world. The MP-5s and AK-56s. I was very much scared but also brave enough to face them. And that was when my fears were answered.'

'A head suddenly popped out of the window. It was a bald man. The man looked all directions. Down, right, left and at last up. As soon as he looked up, I leaned against the roof. I was scratched by the uneven surface of it. It pained a lot but I had to control. An excellent camouflage of black suit against the dark brown roof did the work.'

'"No one here Felix", said that bald man.

"Where could have he gone then?" said the other man. I was happy for not being seen. But then another thought clouded me. I had to get out of there, hadn't I?'

'And to add to my worries, I could see the police cars assembling beneath. The two parts of the bridge were down and joined again. There were white lights flashing all around that area. All the guns of the policemen were pointed up towards the tower on which I was standing. I was trembling.'

'And all types of questions started hacking my mind. "Who'll save me?" "How will I get through this situation?" "What will happen to me?" "What will become of me?" and many silly questions. I tried to connect to Mark through the smartwatch but no avail. I was perspiring.'

'My prayers were actually answered soon enough. But in an exactly opposite way I though initially. A booming voice reached my ears. "I'm dead" I thought. But as the booming voice came closer, I realized it was out jet plane. I was so damn happy to see the plane. Then you all know what happened,' and Ian ended his narration.

'The heck of a story it was,' said Malcolm at last, after a long lonely silence.

'Actually yes. Pretty nail biting and an interesting one too,' Kathy said.

'I mean to say that this is an exceptional adventure though an easy one…..'But Katie stopped Mark.

'You call this easy huh?' and she gave him a blazing look and turned towards Ian again. 'I'm sure everything will be alright again.'

'I hope it would be,' spoke up the cryptic Fred once again.

'What do you mean by hope?' asked Louis, puzzled, grabbing the chocolate lying on the table.

'Are you going to speak about all that stuff you were saying some time ago?' asked Kathy, her face freaking out, losing its colors.

Fred started walking once again about the room. 'Yes,' he finally said, 'but in the evening at four thirty sharp. Till then, good afternoon. I'm off to sleep,' and Fred ran out of the room like a panther following him.

'Is that man crazy?' Ian spoke up.

'Well, we don't know nor does he,' said Malcolm, beaming.

'Let's go now guys. Have some rest and meet at four thirty again. Let Ian rest too. He's too tired, isn't he?' said Katie smiling.

'Yes, I am,' Ian said and with a thud, fell onto the pillow and dozed off.

'Thank him when he gets up. He told us the story in that fatigued state,' Louis said. Everyone turned their heads towards him. The fatso spoke up right things only when needed.

'Sure we will,' said Mark and got up. 'Bye guys. I'm off to my room,' and he left.

After him all left one by one. Malcolm was the last one to come out and that too about ten minutes after the second last person had left. There was something fishy going on. Everyone retired.

Everyone gathered in the main balcony of the fifth floor of Katie's apartment. Everyone sat on the special cane chairs made for them. In front of them was a small glass table supported a tire, a colored one. It was four thirty in the evening and the atmosphere was ablaze. After a series of ice cold drinks, Mark spoke up.

'So, Fred was going to tell us about something, right Fred?' he said grinning.

'I hate that silly grin of yours Mark. And yes. I wanted to say something which I would like to start right away. Did anyone hear the news properly?' said Fred.

'Of course we did. We all did see it together,' said Kathy, with an air of assurance.

'I'm not talking about togetherness. You didn't notice one thing.'

'And what was that?" asked the half dozing Ian, leaning back on his chair.

'The helicopter which you shot down wasn't the police's,' he said resuming his seat.

Ian's eyes widened suddenly. Louis put down his glass of blueberry juice. Everyone suddenly became alarmed. What was Fred telling? Has he gone nuts?

'Have you gone nuts?' asked Malcolm at last.

'No, I've not. You all didn't hear what was being said in the news. They were clearly explaining all this when this fatso suddenly interrupted.'

'Call me by my name,' said Louis, a little petrified.

'Yes. The news people said "They (the police) made sure they followed them (the thieves) but they couldn't cope up with the speed of the jet." These were the lines spoken by them,' Fred said and resumed his raspberry juice.

'You mean...........' said Kathy with a wide mouth, 'we were being followed with the help of something else.'

'Someone else, to correct you.'

'And who could that be?' questioned Ian keeping his cool.

'It's all going to be discovered with the help information which Ian will give.'

'Which information!' a startled Ian asked.

'I'm going to ask some questions to you,' said a grave Fred. 'Firstly, describe whatever you saw about that helicopter.'

'That's not a question, firstly,' said Ian making a weird face.

'Leave all lameness now Ian. We're in great danger right now,' Katie said with worry.

'Okay. So, all that I noticed about the helicopter following us was that it was white.'

'There comes our first conclusion, that it wasn't a police helicopter. London police helicopters are blue,' said Fred, taking a sip of his juice.

'And then what I had noticed is that…wait…the men I saw in the helicopter were clean shaven blondes with a good build. But they were in a police uniform. Fred, how can you prove it was the police behind us?'

'Because they said it,' was the clearest answer one could obtain.

Everyone was in a deep state of shock. How could this be possible? Why would someone follow them? Who knew about them? But there was one more question awaiting. A very major question.

'Okay Fred. The helicopter wasn't the police's helicopter. But why did it blast then?' asked Ian suddenly after a shocking silence.

'It blasted?' gaped Louis and Katie in surprise.

'Of course it did. You two were dozing or what?' said Kathy very casually.

'Uh, we don't know,' said Louis.

'More of that later. As for now the mystery lies as for how did the helicopter blast?' asked Fred.

'You know Fred,' said Mark 'some mysteries are good enough to be left in mid way. The answer comes out later but it does. As for now, leave the blast thing. I'm sure we'll lie upon some point connected to this.'

All felt Mark was right. But a spark lit up suddenly again in the mind of Malcolm.

'Hey guys!' he said with enthusiasm in his voice. 'Want to go to see what happened of the helicopter?'

'That was actually the adventure I was talking about,' said Fred, excited.

'But where will you find it?' asked Kathy.

'Right below the place where we shot it,' said Katie, with a grin of nearing victory. One could still see Kathy's confused look.

'The Thames of course,' said Fred.

'Oh!,' she sighed and had a good laugh over it.

'But how should it be executed?' Ian asked.

'Leave all that to me friends.' said Fred. 'As for now, enjoy the pleasure of having to go for another dangerous day in our lives.'

And he raised his glass.

Chapter 6

A Shark Explodes

A white aircraft flew over the cool waters of the Thames at about 10:30 am. London was bright and perfectly blended with the climate. It was broad daylight. He Londoners as usual were ruffling here and there, some going for work, the kids going to play and others for other reasons.

'Ready to jump?' a person asked from the plane.

'Yes cap,' and saying that, a man clad in a scuba diving cum skydiving suit shot out himself from the plane, and into the Thames. The great thing about it was the splash sound wasn't heard because there were hardly any splashes when he fell into the river. The seers adored it.

Under the water went the man. He sank inside. He put on his goggles and idolized the underwater life. He felt the resistant water which compelled him to obediently sway his body as the water did. Then after about 10 seconds he realized he needed to breathe. He soon took out the breathing machine, a small round device which could fit inside your nostril and let you breathe. He did what had to be done and then wriggled a little, out of air, just because he didn't trust that device which Fred had given them.

After gathering much courage he decided to breathe through his nostrils. He was sure that the water would gush up to his lungs. But he was wrong. Ian could easily breathe. He sighed, feeling relaxed. All this duration his eyes were closed. Now he opened them. He glanced upon the surface of the river. He could clearly see the golden sunlight penetrating through the river surface. That color blend seemed beautiful to him. Soon, one by one five more black figures emerged in front of his eyes like a drop of black paint put in a crystal clear bowl of water. All of them were wriggling for breath. Ian gestured to relax and breathe. All the five human-fish were pacified after they breathed. All their uncomfort vanished.

'Which way now?' asked Louis.

Yes! They were talking through radio. Advanced tech. And on top of everything, their voice sounded too clear.

'Where did the helicopter fall?' Ian asked to the others.

'It's two and a half kilometers away from the Tower bridge,' answered Katie.

'And are we?' asked Fred.

'Shut up Fred. I've steered the plane right on the spot,' said Louis.

'And you left the plane in whose hands?' asked a very surprised Ian.

'Mark,' said Kathy.

'Does he know how to drive a plane?'

'Yeah. I mean no. I mean….. he said he could,' said Malcolm.

"Okay then. Let's advance. C'mon guys, everyone dive down,' said Ian and at once all started.

As they started the background around them was the blend of the sunlight with the water with a very few fish and lots of waste materials. But as they descended deeper, the fish increased, going around in shoals. The surrounding turned cobalt blue. The fishes were looking extremely beautiful and underwater was like magic for them. It was great down there. But it was getting colder and colder too. And dark. So everyone switched on their torches.

All were going down together but Katie suddenly lost her velocity. She lagged behind suddenly. She was sensing danger. All the others moved on. It was after a few seconds that they realized that Katie wasn't with them.

'Hey! Katie? Where are you?' Malcolm sent a message to her.

'Right above you guys.'

'Then come down. What're you doing up there?'

'I'm sensing some danger is going to approach very soon.'

'Philosophy later, now come down and ……..' but Katie cut him off in mid-sentence.

'Yeah Malcolm. There's danger already. Look to your right everyone,' she screamed.

All looked towards their right. Something was seen. It was faintly seen for it was very far and the lights couldn't travel that much.

'That might be a submarine,' spoke up Louis.

'Where do you see submarines in rivers Louis?' asked Ian with an exasperated tone

'Okay. Enough of it, both of you,' said Kathy. 'Let the thing come near first.'

After 7-8 seconds, the thing was almost clearly visible. They stopped dead. They turned white all over. It was like sweating even in water. Hard to believe but it was a hammerhead shark.

It stopped at a distance first and stared at its food. Six fleshy humans easily available! Wow. It slowly proceeded further and started circling them like a hungry wolf.

'I've much knowledge about these......' Fred started but Kathy cut him off.

'Arrive at the point,' she said in a panicked voice.

'It will go at a distance and then after waiting for 2-3 seconds it will charge. On my count of three dive down at the fullest speed,'

The shark then suddenly swam past them and stopped at a distance. And as Fred said it did charge.

'One...'

'Two...'

'Three...'

And everyone dived at the fullest speed. Malcolm had said something in panic which the others couldn't hear clearly.

And as Fred had said it had charged them. It was overhauling all the professionally trained swimmers. But they were not so easily to be defeated. They took a series a of turns and hauls and tricked the shark into overturning its brain.

But swimming and saving themselves from the shark didn't seem a good option for it was faster than them. And then the miracle took place.

Suddenly, in the midst of all the confusion, the special devices named 'Hydrosubs' sloshed into the river. It was a device specially made just for them. It contained of a round circular 14 inch platform attached to a black colored, adjustable rod out of which's ends stuck out two handles for holding it. And there was a black colored device attached to the rod containing the GPS and three buttons. Red for boost, green for converting it into a jetpack and yellow for strapping the rider's legs when at a very high speed.

The six computer powered hydrosubs directed themselves towards the six friends, each hydrosub on each person. Everyone rode their hydrosub and set of zooming in the underwater.

They drove the hydrosubs quite professionally. Louis tried a deadly stunt. He went near the blood thirsty shark and as he was approaching it, he directed his hydrosub up, in the direction of the river's surface. Then within a second he turned around, took out his gun and shot precisely at the shark.

Bang!

He missed.

'Guys! Guys! The shark's disappeared suddenly,' Malcolm said.

'It might be tired,' Kathy said.

'Don't joke around there fools,' Louis said. 'The shark's here with me.'

'What do you mean by "with me"? Are you playing with it?' Ian asked.

'Wait Louis, I'm coming to help,' and saying that Fred scurried towards Louis's course.

When he reached there, it was long way. Louis and the shark had moved far, fighting. And then what he saw was unbelievable. Louis was almost falling to the shark after a long chase and catch with it.

Fred super sped his hydrosub directly towards Louis. He was still a few meters far from them. He pressed the yellow button. The straps came out from the platform and held his legs and the hydrosub zoomed like a Ferrari. Louis was nearing the shark's mouth now.

Fred held out his hand now and tilted the hydrosub.

'Louis!' he yelled, 'grab my hand.'

Fred was just in time to save Louis. Louis stretched out his hand and grabbed Fred's hand. Fred, with all his might swung Louis onto his back and sped in the direction where the others were.

'Fred,' Louis said in his petrified voice, 'I want to go near the shark. Once.'

'Are you mad my friend,' Fred asked in bewilderment.

'Please my friend, just once,' Louis pleaded.

'Okay but we'll die together, if we do,' Fred said.

'We won't. It's the matter of just two seconds,' Louis said, fatigue still audible in his voice.

Fred steered at full speed in the direction of the shark. They had reached too far from it. They saw the shark from a distance. It was squirming continuously.

'Good time, speed up,' Louis said.

Fred steered the hydrosub towards the shark and in moments they were there, right against the shark. See them, the shark raged and let out a fierce growl.

This was the time Louis had waited for. He took out his gun and swiftly aimed and shot two bullets directly in the centre of the mouth. And then they fled in their friends' direction.

Soon they were at a considerable distance from the shark. Fred kept speeding but Louis looked back while still on Fred's back.

The shark now started wriggling furiously. It vibrated and vibrated. And suddenly it exploded with a forceful blast. A great ball of fire erupted and spread in all directions. The strong gale charged out of the fireball rushed everywhere. Louis and Fred were thrown many meters into the direction they were going, with its force. And eventually they reached to their friends faster.

Louis was totally bewildered to see it. His suspicions were true. Just his suspicions. He did not get the story. What actually was going on. Nothing could be understood.

Soon they reached where the others were. Everyone was engrossed in looking at something. Fred helped Louis to get onto the hydrosub.

'What are they looking at?' Louis questioned too gradually.

'Well, that was a massive explosion. Didn't they hear it?'

'Right. It may be possible that they've not heard it because we're underwater.'

'But wait,' said Fred, and grinned, 'I think Louis, we're already reached the bottom of this deep sea.'

'Are you serious?' asked Louis going white all over.

'Yeah. Step down. It's the sand bed,' said Fred.

Louis did as told. He heaved a sigh of relief.

'But,' he asked, 'our question is what are these guys Looking over to?'

At the same time Ian turned back. He had heavy stress on his face.

'Oh! Thank God both of you've come,' he said. 'Look here,' and he invited them to see what the others were seeing.

Fred and Louis both went forward to have a look.

'Your suspicions were smart like you Fred,' Kathy said while they were still advancing.

'But what is it?' asked a frustrated Louis.

Both came and saw what had troubled them with a shower of questions.

There lay the large fragments of the remains of the white colored aviation transport which was the nightmare of their lives after the robbery of the Kohinoor. The thing which they assumed to be of the police. The thing that had defied them. The thing that had put them in the danger of facing a shark. Here was the helicopter which blasted when Ian had shot the pilot.

'Whoa,' Louis backed off. 'Where and how....... I mean how did you find this?'

'It wasn't difficult,' Malcolm said. 'Ian asked where was the spot where the helicopter had blasted. Katie the all knower said it was around 2km from the Tower Bridge. And as fate would permit it we were right in the spot.'

'And how did you know that?'

'We have a GPS with us,' Kathy said.

'Oh yeah,' said Fred smiling but in a matter of seconds became serious. 'You started looking and searching for this thing while I was gone and Louis was in danger? How could you do that?'

'All Ian's idea. He was too fast. He wanted everything fast isn't it?' Katie said in a sarcastic tone.

'Sorry for that Fred,' Ian said.

'No need for it. Can we advance to excavating this thing now?'

'Oh sure!' said Kathy and grabbed the biggest fragment of the broken helicopter. 'C'mon Fred. Help me out.'

Fred swam over to Kathy swiftly and Helped her to move the fragment to the side.

'We need more help,' said Fred. Malcolm and Ian rushed over to help them. The fragile Katie and the delicate Kathy stood out of it, Kathy switching places with Louis.

After apply a brutal amount of energy, they were able to move that thing and that too after Malcolm had cut the pieces into two using the deadly laser watch on his wrist which emitted laser.

'Well well. What do we get after moving a mountainous fragment? Two more fragments enclosed like a door,' Louis said, irritated. 'Oh my, I'm so tired.'

'Yes. Louis has had a rough day today' said Fred.

'Huh?' mewled Malcolm.

'More of that later. Louis, have rest,' Fred said, soothing Louis from the influence of the dreadful event.

'Sit?! There's no place to sit here Fred,' Malcolm said.

'I never said to sit. I just told him to relax. Go and stand beside those girls Louis,' Fred replied growling at Malcolm's misunderstood sentence.

Louis went over to where the girls stood, hunched down.

Meanwhile the three friends resumed their work of removing the other fragments of the helicopter. As they removed the first one, they saw a jar of Dairy Milk chocolates but with lack of chocolates. Inside was a piece of paper, rolled and pale. It was pretty large in size and seemed as if compressed inside the jar.

'What's this thing doing down here?' wondered Fred, Malcolm and Ian while Malcolm picked it up from its half-dug-into-the-ground position.

'I can't see it properly,' said Fred taking the jar from Malcolm's and holding it up to examine it. 'Treasure Island,' he said and chuckled.

'Keep that thing in the bag,' Ian said. 'We'll have a look at it after we reach.'

The told was done.

'Remove the other piece guys,' Katie said, wondering what they were talking about and what had they found.

'Wait a second. We're on it now,' said a little irritated Ian.

And the three friends began moving the third piece. When they had removed it, there was a plain blank expression on everyone's face. What they saw before their eyes was just empty ground, like a deadpan. Nothing there below the helicopter fragments. They just stared at each other's faces.

'Where are the corpses?' Kathy said, terrified.

'Yes. Exactly. Where are the corpses?' said Katie too, going white all over.

'Do you expect the whole bodies of the corpses to be found after the helicopter has exploded?' Louis said sensibly.

'Excuse me robotics, what?' Malcolm asked sarcastically.

'The bodies must have been reduced to ashes my friends, when it blasted, the helicopter.'

Everyone let out a loud whooooooo.

'Fatso has said something sensible today,' grinned Ian. 'How did you think of this?'

'Something's fishy,' Fred said under his breath.

'What Fred?' asked Kathy.

'No. Nothing,' he replied with a broad smile.

'Good. Now let's go back up,' Louis said.

'No,' said Fred. The bodies ought to be here somewhere.'

'It's no use looking now Fred. Robotics has said they must have been reduced to ashes,' Malcolm tried to convince.

'We can't give up so easily,' Fred said, a little flamed up. 'We've come for that particular reason. We can't leave without accomplishing it.'

'Well actually you're right Fred,' Ian said. 'But we got to leave. Louis's reason is sensibly and logically very much right.'

'Okay. I respect your decisions but let us take a one last look,' Fred pleaded.

Knowing it was no use to preside his argument over Fred's, Ian told everyone to have a last look around the place.

Everyone started looking around, though not in a mood to look. After a few moments Kathy saw something glimmering against the blue background of the underwater. It was dug in the sand and red light was constantly sparkling. She cleared the sandy part above the object and dislodged it. It was a spherical metal ball of around a fist's size. On the middle of the ball was engraved "Beware".

'Look guys. I found something,' said Kathy and held up the sphere.

Everyone glanced in her direction.

'Same here.'

'Same here!'

The other two people were Katie and Ian. They too had found the same metal sphere which Kathy held in her hand. On their spheres too, "Beware" was engraved in bold letters.

And as everyone looked on, the red light suddenly started glimmering all the more.

'Kathy,' bellowed Fred and swam up to her as fast as he could. He grabbed the sphere from her hands and dug it back into the sand.

'Ian, Katie, drop it,' he said hastily.

'What's the matter?' Katie asked.

'I'll tell you later. Just dig that thing in the ground.'

Ian and Katie panicked. They half dug it and then Fred gave his orders.

'Mount your hydrosubs everyone.'

Everyone did as they were told.

'To the fullest speed.'

Everyone pressed the yellow button. The straps held their legs firmly and their hydrosubs sped off like a rocket, to the surface of the river.

After fractions of a second, they could see a huge, expanding orange hot ball spread under the water, advancing towards them with a rapid rate. Within moments the orange huge ball and the six friends had reached the surface simultaneously. And the orange ball exploded after coming in contact with the air and shot up a vertical and a powerful jet of water, high into the sky.

And with that it flung up high into the air, the six friends. They let themselves loose for seconds, feeling powerless. Everyone pressed then, the red button, also known for allowing the hydrosubs soar into the air. It opened thin and Herculean flaps with boosters. They were now soaring high into the air.

'Mark, where's our jet?' Ian said out of panic.

'Well, I'm sorry guys but the plane is out of order right now. I'm fixing it,' Mark replied.

'Guys, we've no option now. Use the jetpacks to go to the house,' Ian said.

'We don't have them,' a worried Louis said.

'The green button everybody,' Katie said.

Everyone immediately pressed the green button. The hydrosubs converted into jetpacks. The 14 inch platform moved itself to the backside of everyone like a bad and the rod split into two thinner rods attached to the platform. Two red buttons emerged out of them. They pressed the left red button and they were off.

After some time, they landed in the lawn of their house. They took of their jetpacks, completely stupefied an exhausted. They stormed into the house and occupied their own rooms and sunk into their beds, deep in slumber.

Chapter 7

The Jar

'The "Au" Island.'

'The which island, Kathy?' asked Louis sulking on the sofa, eating a cheesecake.

And there they all were, leaning over the piece of paper they'd found in the jar. It was a pretty long and broad paper. The material being stiff. All over the pale paper nothing was written except for the title of the paper. The "Au" Island. And then there was a certain map drawn with directions to something.

'What could it be?' asked Fred to the others, leaving Louis on the sofa.

'Anyone ready to be Sherlock?' asked a totally confused Ian.

'All of us,' said Mark and they started concentrating on the paper rather map, to deduce whatever little they could.

After they came, they went into deep slumber, fatigued from the two mysterious life threatening adventures. The attack of the shark and the unexpected exploding of the unanticipated found three metal spheres. After they got up they assembled in the main hall downstairs and didn't speak a word to each other. For about an hour they all remained dumb and tried to recover from the shock that had come upon them. All were gloomy and despised. It was Mark who broke the silence.

'So, tell me about your interesting journey downstairs… Sorry, underwater,' with a wide smile.

'Well, thanks Mark making me remember but Fred would you please bring the paper we found inside the Dairy Milk jar underwater?' Ian said with a disoriented voice.

Fred got up to bring his bag.

'Seriously? Are you kidding?' Mark said.

Kathy glance him a fiery look.

'I mean you found a jar of Dairy Milk with no chocolates in it but a paper. Wow! How cool is that,' he clarified himself.

'Too cool Mark. And please shut up for some moments. We're really worried here,' Katie said frustrated. He folded and hand and leaned back on the sofa.

In the meanwhile Fred came with one hand searching for the jar in the bag.

'Here it is,' he said and took out the jar for everyone to see. He walked over to the table and set the jar there. 'If you want to see, here it is. I'm opening it.'

'Go ahead Fred,' Malcolm said and everybody except Louis got up to have a look of what was there.

Suddenly Katie spoke up, 'It looks like a pretty old paper piece.'

'And that's what Katie has deduced. Anyone else would like to have a try?' Ian said, half sarcastic, half meaning what he said.

'I want to,' Louis said, raising his hand with cheesecake stuffed in his mouth. 'It might be a trick. Could be possible colored.'

'Prove it,' Mark said.

'Dab some wet cotton on it and see if the color spreads its influence on the cotton ball,' Louis said, grinning all the while.

'You do it,' Mark argued.

'Well, you want a proof, don't you? Therefore you do it,' Louis said and relaxed again.

'That fatso might be right. Let's check,' Ian said. 'Mark, please do the needful. As Louis said.'

Mark scowled at Louis and went and brought a wet piece of cotton quickly.

'Dab it. Go on,' Louis said.

Mark dabbed the cotton on the edges of the paper and yes, the color came off.

'Damn! He was right,' Fred said. 'Good teamwork Kathy and Louis.'

Louis raised his glass of coke. 'Thanks,' he said and took a sip.

'Well, we would like more deductions. Anyone more,' Ian asked.

'Hey. Wait Ian. Are you auctioning deductions?' asked Fred.

'No, Why.'

'Then why the auctioning tone?'

'Oh,' Ian smiled, 'just like that.'

'Wait. I know something,' Kathy spoke up.

'What?'

'I just know that this thing was kept there below the helicopter fragments just for us to find,' she said, trembling all over.

'Are you scared for something might come upon us?' asked Fred.

'Yes,' she said. 'And this thing is also maybe a riddle to be solved. And I have a feeling in my bones that we're going to crack this thing only if we follow the route of the map given here.'

'Yes but……. what did you say?' Malcolm said.

'I have a feeling in my bones that we're going to crack this thing only if we follow the route of the map given here.'

'Exactly. We have to follow the route given in the map,' Malcolm said with a gist of pride having cracked a part of the puzzle.

'Bravo,' Fred told to Malcolm.

'Bravo to girl power Fred. The girls have discovered and given us the clues,' Malcolm said, saying this he gave all the credit to the girls.

'But what about the map coordinates? We don't have them do we?' Mark questioned suddenly.

'That is a question to pound over. Absolutely right Mark,' Louis said.

'I'm going to have rest. It's almost night,' Louis said ruffling his hair.

'It's not six thirty in the evening yet Louis,' Mark said.

'That's why I said it's almost night,' and he chuckled. 'Good night.'

'Hey! What about dinner?' Kathy asked. 'We're going to Palazzo's Pizza Palace for dinner.'

'I've had mine. Don't force me for dinner now. Bye. Enjoy. Take rest. Good night,' and he slammed the door behind him.

'That was too many wishes before going to bed, right?' Ian asked turning around to everyone.

Everyone nodded.

'Wake up Louis, it's ten thirty in the morning,' Fred said, opening the curtains so the bright radiant sunlight would fall directly on Louis' face.

'Why so early?'

Fred went out of his room and told the others

'He's not waking up saying it's too early to wake up?'

Everyone gaped.

'You told him it's ten thirty?' asked Kathy.

'I did and that is when he said, "Why so early".'

'My my. Leave him. Let's go. We're getting late,' Katie said.

'We need him, at least today. Didn't you see the way he deduced things yesterday?'

'Okay. Go call him,' Kathy complied.

Fred stormed into Louis's room once again.

'Get up and freshen up yourself fast. We're leaving for the Tate Modern. We'll see historical things and artifacts and…….'

'Hold on. Tate Modern? I'm coming,' Louis said and rushed to freshen up.

Fred walked out of the room and conveyed the thumbs up sign.

'Good,' said Ian. 'Mark ain't coming. He's going to fix the plane.'

'Louis too can do that,' Katie said.

'But we need Louis and Mark is the only next person we can depend upon to have the plane fixed. He gave that idea, I didn't force it on him. Now done with reasons?' Ian asked turning towards Kathy.

'Yeah well,' she said giving a forceful smile. 'Thanks.'

After about twenty minutes, Louis came out of the room.

'We're ready to go guys,' he said, caressing his cream colored suit.

'Great dressing Louis but we aren't going for the queen's dinner,' Malcolm said. Everyone giggled.

'Now let's move,' Ian said and they all stepped out of the house.

Chapter 8

Solution To The Riddle

After about six hours or so, the six friends who'd gone to visit the Tate modern returned, not to their house in London but back to Germany, Dublin. They all were not what they went as. All of them were clad in black clothes, the scuba cum skydiving suits. They went up in Kathy's building. All were so worn out, powerless even to pick a glass of water themselves. And the events which had come upon them and the latest one today compelled them to think and figure out what was exactly going on in their life. The past four days were totally like inferno.

Who is behind these scenes? Who knows about our plans? And about the incident at the Tate, who knew we were going to be there? And that too today? The questions were creating a murderous mystery in the minds.

Everyone thwacked themselves onto the sofas. Mark had already reached there. These friends had already contacted him, telling him to reach Dublin as fast as possible. He brought in the juices and water for them.

'Care for some?' Mark asked, while settling himself on the sofa.

Malcolm moved his hand sideways, gesturing a no. Everyone was deep in thought, eyes wide with astonishment and a humorless expression prevailing on their features.

Mark shrugged his shoulders and picked up the book lying on the table beside him and started reading it. A very long string of silence followed. After an hour or so, Ian suddenly erupted.

'Anyone getting any clue about the stranger?' with a sharp look.

'Stranger? What stranger?' asked Mark.

'Please remain quiet Mark. We'll tell you everything later,' a frustrated Fred said.

'He was so ridiculous,' Malcolm said, 'like … how … I can't understand.'

'He already knows about it. He said it himself,' Kathy said.

'Knows what? Please let me know guys,' Mark pleaded.

'Wait Mark,' Katie said again and toppled him off.

'Wait a second everyone,' said Kathy, picking up an apple while getting up and walked over to the balcony. 'Doesn't everything seem strange. Everything. One instant we are being followed by an unknown helicopter. And then when we go to decode the mystery, we're saved from being devoured by a shark and dying due to a metal sphere with glimmering red lights. And then today's incident. And the map which we obtained today,' she said pointing to the piece of paper kept on the table.

Mark got up and had a look at it from a distance.

'It's the same one isn't it?'

'No. It is a different one,' Fred said.

'Can't be,' Mark said and jumped towards the table. 'Yeah,' observing the map. 'It has map coordinates too.'

'And that person has already provided us clues. How much stranger could this be?' Ian said, scratching his head.

'What clues?'

'Never mind. We'll tell you everything later.'

'Oh!' Mark grunted and resumed his seat.

'All this seems sort of connected,' Katie spoke.

'Well, it might be,' Malcolm said. And dead silence followed again.

'Hey people, look,' Louis said breaking the silence. 'Forget the past, plan for the future but with the tip obtained by that man.'

'But what can we infer from the map? Nothing,' Ian said sarcastically, ruffling his hair.

'Malcolm got up and walked over to the map. He observed it for about a minute and then asked,

'Who's the scientist here?'

Fred and Louis looked at each other and then raised their hands.

'And who's much into chemistry?'

Louis directed his hand towards Fred. Fred reddened.

'Well, I am much of a physicist but chemistry somewhat I know,' he said, smiling.

'Could you then please take the trouble of coming over here and telling me something?'

All eyes towards Fred now.

'Don't stare at me like that. I'm going,' he said and stood up and went over to the table.

'What do you infer from the title of the map?' asked Malcolm, pointing towards the heading.

'Well, The "Au" island,' he said interrogatively. 'What does it have anything to do with chemistry?"

'Well, I want to know because I don't know, what does "Au" depict in chemistry?'

'Well,' Fred said. Everyone was waiting from an answer out of him, directly gazing at him. ' "Au" stands for…' he thought for a minute and spoke up with delight.

' "Au" stands for the element Gold. Yes! We decoded the title at least,' and he punched his fist in the air.

'Well deduced Fred and yes, Malcolm too,' said Ian as everybody got up in the happiness of solving the root of the mystery.

'But, but,' said Louis, 'the map has to say something related to gold.'

'Easy fatso. It is a treasure map. We're going to be the next Jim Hawkins. Treasure Island,' Katie said and chuckled.

'Okay. So you guys intend to go as per the map and fetch the gold from wherever it is, right?' asked Mark with a crooked expression.

'Great idea Mark,' Ian said, his face lightning up.

'Hey hey. I was asking. I didn't suggest,' Mark clarified himself.

'But in the process of asking, you already suggested it and we like the idea,' Malcolm said.

'But..'

'No buts. Great work Mark,' Fred said. Mark sat down in disappointment.

'And what about the other plans? The helping of Indian people and stuff?' asked Katie.

'I've already thought of it,' Ian answered. 'We retrieve the gold and in that way help the Indian poor.'

'Great thinking Robin Hood,' said Fred, pouring himself a glass of his favorite apple juice.

'The journey's gonna be a perilous one,' said Kathy.

'But who's going to be the geologist now?' Louis asked.

'Meaning?' Fred asked.

'We know the coordinates but which place exactly? We need to find,' he said.

He's right, everyone thought. We need to know the place.

'Look here,' Mark said, moving his hand over the map. On the top left corner of the backside of the map, in very small fonts was written "700 km off the Bombay coast".

Ian went over and brightened up.

'Yessss!' He shot up. 'We know the exact location,' and he jumped into the air.

'Woah! Woah! Easy Ian,' Katie said. 'And great discovering Mark.'

'My pleasure,' he replied.

'That means we will have to go to Bombay? Isn't it?' said Kathy with a gist of excitement. Mark and Ian on the floor, all subdued in thought suddenly. "Bombay?" They thought. "The place of the most crazy people existing. And what do we do there?"

'Right. We make all our contacts from there about all stuff regarding ammunition and other things we'll need on the journey,' Katie said.

'You've decided on the journey already?' Mark asked raising his eyebrow.

'Of course I have. We are going to get the gold to ourselves after all.'

'Great decision Katie,' Louis said. 'And one more thing for you guys. You'll be surprised but I also know how to steer and handle a cruise liner,' he said blushing.

'Wow! Louis, that is exciting news. Now we won't need any ship driver,' Kathy said.

'Well deduced Kathy. We will go in a ship. That is what I meant by saying I know how to drive a ship.'

'You have made great plans in one instant guys. Bravo,' and Malcolm raised his apple juice glass.

And all were almost so happy to embark upon now another journey. That too a treasure one. Their dream had spread itself out of the books. Ecstasy prevailed upon them. They just had to take care of the Bombay crowd. Above ten million people in just 603 sq km. Too amazing.

'Great work everyone. All of us. This is going to be a rocking journey. Imagine, we seven friends on a ship and then on the island and we're searching for the gold all over the island in groups and……..'

But Katie cut Fred off. Louis and she looked towards each other. Something was wrong.

'Keep your hair on guys,' Louis said suddenly after silence totally dwelled.

'Shut up fatso,' said an irritated Katie.

Yes. They were right. All of them could hear some voice. It was getting louder as more silence fell when the glasses stopped tinkling on the table. It was a voice making some kind of countdown.

Tick! Tick! Tick!

Katie got up and started searching for the source of the sound. It wasn't easy to sense it that too on the top floor of the building. She went all over the drawing room.

Nothing was found. Then she tried the top floor kitchen. Nothing there too. She opened the jars and checked the pipe leakage. No problem with them. She looked up then in the bedrooms. She checked all of them, in vain.

At last, she reached her own room. The voice was indeed, the loudest here. She surveyed the room with the ultra powerful eyes. And there it was. On the milk white colored door of the cupboard, a black object containing some wires and spiral wires was fit. A small orange rectangular screen did the countdown.

Katie turned white. She just couldn't believe what she saw in front of her. She rushed out of the bedroom and screamed.

'Get out of here as fast as you can,' and she immediately scrambled the hydrosubs by going over to the closet behind the television and pressing the secret concealed button there. Immediately the wall to their left moved revealing the colossal amount of technology they had stored there. Laptops computers, and scientific gadgets and everything they found fascinating on the earth was stored there.

As the wall moved open, seven hydrosubs zoomed out. Everyone ducked to save themselves from being hurt by the hydrosubs.

'Mount them,' Kathy said.

'But what is the matter?' Ian said at the top of his voice against the din caused by the hydrosubs.

'All later,' Kathy said pleading, 'please get onto the hydrosubs and out of the building as fast as you can.'

'Everyone except her mounted and hydrosubs.

'Where to now?' Louis asked.

'Follow me,' Ian said and they activated the soaring option of the hydrosub. All followed him out of the great window and into the air and soared high enough to have a whole top and side view of the building. Everyone made a huge circle.

'Are we gonna hang like this in until she calls us back in?' Louis asked, being acrophobic.

'Eventually yes,' Ian replied.

Up above them was the pitch black sky, with glistening spots of silver all over it. Below was the city of Dublin, illuminated in white streetlights and the yellow lights of the moving vehicles. Luckily for them to enable to see, Kathy's building's corners too had four bright white lights.

'Can anybody tell me what is going on here?' Katie asked feeling afraid.

'Not a single idea about it,' Mark said perspiring all over.

'Neither me,' Ian said, adjusting his hair, balancing the hydrosub on one hand.

It was Fred then, who on top of all troubles added one more. He lowered his hydrosub and in the direction of Kathy's bedroom window. And then he tried to barge inside the bedroom through the window but it was closed. He was banging his hand repeatedly on the glass pane trying to ask what was going on.

'What are you doing there, you lunatic?' Mark shouted and everyone drove their hydrosubs over to him.

'Look everyone,' he said pointing his finger towards the bedroom. 'Kathy's still in there.'

And no one believed what they saw. She was the only one inside the building and was trying to do something with a scissors and protective gloves.

'She's trying to deactivate a bomb,' Louis screamed, petrified.

'Hey! Kathy,' Fred now shouted, banging harder than before. Kathy suddenly grabbed attention. She ran over to the window and opened it. A gust of air blew in. Fred somersaulted inside. 'What're you doing?' he said.

'I got to save my house,' she said, panicking.

'But now just 30 seconds are left,' Fred said. 'Do what you want, fast?'

Kathy ran over to the bomb and tried fully to deactivate it.

'Kathy! Leave it,' Fred screamed.

20, 19, 18.

Fred ran over to Kathy and started pleading her to stop. Six seconds elapsed.

12, 11, 10.

She didn't lose hope. She reached at deactivating point of taking out the main metal part.

10, 9, 8, 7.

The metal suddenly got stuck, unwilling to come out.

6, 5, 4.

'Kathy, come out,' the others cried out loud.

Fred held her by the hand and darted for the window, while one of her hand still fidgeting to take the metal out.

3.

'Leave me.'

2.

'No Kathy.' And they were about to reach the window.

1.

Kathy held on to Fred at the window and both of them bent, not knowing what will happen the next second and waiting for the house to explode.

'I'm alive,' Kathy shouted in horror.

'Of course you are,' Fred said from beside her.

'You too...'

'Yes.'

'But how did this happen?' Kathy said helping herself a glass of water from the table kept beside the bed where she and Fred lay.

We weren't aware of anything actually. When will the bomb explode? When will you come out? And many other questions bothered us. We waited for around ten minutes but you two didn't come out nor did you wake up,' Fred gave the explanation.

'Hang on,' Fred said. 'You're saying you waited for ten minutes and that the bomb didn't explode? How cool is that?' he turned towards Kathy.

'Well. I've seen considerable amount of movies which have these kinds of thrills. So I kind of dared to come inside and find what had happened. And I did get to understand that much, that the metal part which deactivates the bomb had come out,' Malcolm said.

'I liked that story,' Kathy said sarcastically. 'And how did that happen?' she said with a wicked grin.

'As I deduced,' Louis spoke up, 'from the scratches on the metal part in which the metal deactivator was placed, I can say that it was stuck very badly when pulled with much external force and it came out due to some "Occasional" external force. Maybe it was the time when Fred was pulling Kathy and she was struggling to take it out. That was the occasional force. And when Kathy was struggling to take the metal out by herself before Fred entered, the metal might have got stuck due to extensive force. This is the only logical explanation I can provide,' and he poured himself a glass of juice kept there on the table.

'Well deduced Louis,' said Malcolm, slapping him on the back.

'Then where exactly are we?' Kathy asked keeping her hand on her forehead, trying to recall, still subconscious.

'We're in your building and in Fred's room. The best part for you,' Katie smiled and said.

Kathy heaved a sigh of relief. She then turned to look at the clock.

12:30am.

'Too late in the night,' Ian said yawning a bit.

'Good night everyone. I'm off to sleep,' Mark said and vanished like vapor.

'Good night Fred, Kathy and everyone. I'm totally weary today. I'll be needing rest,' Malcolm said. Fred nodded.

'Same here,' Ian said.

'And same here too. I need to recover from the shock,' Kathy smiled and said, 'Good night Fred.'

And one by one, Fred's room got deserted. Fred thumped back on the bed again, wondering how the day had passed like. Totally like in the grave mystery on the Hound of the Baskervilles.

And the night wore on. The sun had hidden itself in the phantom of the dark night long ago. Dublin, while still illuminated, sank into the darkness. The population had retired for the night. The night flowers thrived and the ones which had blossomed, budded. The seven friends their closed their eyes to liberate the fatigue in them. The day had come to an end. Who knew what was going to happen further? No one even had a hint of tomorrow. All slept soundly.

Chapter 9

Fish Fantasy

The blue waters of the Arabian sea splashed upon its own waves, sweeping a large area of the sea. The atmosphere was very cool. The colossal sea expressed a wish of elegance. The underground ocean current vibrated so strongly as to shake someone's within. The marine life was merry and joyous inside. The seahorses danced, the starfish rested, the clownfish toured in shoals and the dolphins jumped in ecstasy. Seagulls soared high over the gigantic water body to hunt for prey. Far away a landmass was spotted, big and nugget shaped. All over the landmass it was just greenery that flourished. Trees and trees and trees. An island which was green and great.

At some distance from the island, an enormous ship was sighted. The body made of steel and a blue colored strip at the bottom of the ship against the white color of the entire ship. A suite of rooms decorated the wide upper deck of the ship. The mast was high up, flapping the white flag with a red colored symbol of the index finger and the middle finger making a "V" symbolizing victory.

The ship was equipped with all kinds of modern technologies. All that was needed to survive with and all that was needed to be protected with.

The front part of the deck contained a pool of water as every ship contains. Warm water. The polished light brown extra smooth floor of the ship made it look even more rich and pleasurable. The other delights of the ship were the all time food court, the ballroom, the cinema, and the ultra modern suites. Just everything a man needed to live all his life.

A man lay there, beside the pool on his beach chair. He had on his swimwear and brown sunglasses with a beach umbrella specially kept there for shade. On the table beside him was kept a glass of pineapple juice and some garnished Italian salad. He lay there sunbathing himself, hands folded and behind his head.

'It's great to be here,' he muttered to himself.

Just then another man entered the scene. He was in a perfect formal costume, clad in black and wore black robot-type sunglasses. The man sunbathing himself looked up to see who it was.

'Oh! It's you. We're not here in our business meeting. Come and have a seat here,' he indicated towards the beach chair beside him.

After a great deal of silence the other man spoke up.

'Is it the time to rest now?'

'Why that question suddenly?' the first man asked.

'Because we're nearing the island now. Just six kilometers left now.'

'Hold on then,' the first man said getting up. 'I'm going to freshen up. You wait here,' and saying this he vanished into the suites.

After about ten minutes, the man who now was beside the pool opened the GPS and saw the distance that was left. Five kilometers, it showed.

And out of the blue, suddenly two Spitfires appeared from among the green trees of the island. The two powerful front rotors made a sturdy buzzing voice. The green and off-white jets were just a sight to look at. One of them had a big "V-10" written on it and the other one had a "V-19" written on it in the same way.

The man in the suit looked around to look the Spitfires. "Great sight at an isolated place," he thought. "We're not the only ones here." But then what he saw was unthinkable. The planes were heading directly towards their ship. He ran at the man's suite and started banging the door.

'Come out. Two spitfires are heading at us. Our ship.'

'What is a spitfire?' the man asked opening the door.

'Fighter jets,' the other man said. 'We ought to hide now.'

'Our rooms should be the best place for that,' the man said, still wondering what was so terrifying about the Spitfires.

Both men rushed to their own suites. After ten minutes, they heard the banging of the bullets on the deck of the ship. The bullet marks made in the wood were clearly visible to them. And then they heard the sound of bullets striking off the metal parts of the ship.

Clang! Clang!

The next few minutes were the years of hell of them. What was happening? Who are shooting? Why are they shooting? What crime did we commit? Is he a business rival? Or a stranger person?

In the midst of all these thoughts, they saw something indefinable fall from the planes. Something black and hard.

The next second saw just orange fire erupting out of the ship. The ship was reduced to ashes.

Two corpses shifted down deep into the waters of the Arabian sea.

'600km from Bombay. 100km to go,' the computer said.

'That's cool,' the seasick Louis said. 'Just 100 more kilometers of sickness. And then it's all over.'

'Remain on bed fatty acid. Or we'll have to call a bulldozer to get you out of this ship,' Fred said and the others giggled.

'Dare you anything like that again,' Louis said furiously.

'He's kidding Louis,' Ian said. 'Don't fume.'

And there they were all, at the food court. It was bright morning outside the ship in which the seven friends were traveling. The sunshine didn't show any signs of mercy to lower its intensity. The seagulls soared around and small fish jumped in and out of the water again and again, relishing the sunlight.

They had all supported the seasick Louis in coming to the food court by holding his body. And then they thumped him onto the widest chair available. Louis was actually seasick. Having travelled from a few days he couldn't resist the desire to complete the journey as fast as possible.

'Shoals of fishes are seen underwater at this point,' the computer beeped suddenly. 'Clown fishes and seahorses will remain the most elegant sight for the rest of the journey. The other delights here include dolphins and other small fishes.'

Ian, a fish fanatic, on hearing this, soon rushed down the stair from the deck. There downstairs he arrived at the "Sight room" specially made for having a glance at the underwater life through a wide and a long piece of thick, sturdy and clear transparent glass. He quickly went over the glass and started adoring the underwater life.

Meanwhile, on the deck, Kathy lay there, flipping through the pages of "The Amazing Sights of the Royal Sea".

'Dolphins are not bound to be found on this sight,' she said after some time, still flipping through the book's pages.

'Books say anything,' Louis said while in bed. 'For instance…'

'Now don't start that story of yours about Harry Potter connected to the real world. That's called fiction,' Katie said annoyingly.

'I'd prefer friction,' Louis said and laughed out loud.

'Good try scientist but that was a lame joke,' Kathy said.

'Hey! Everyone! Come down here,' Ian bellowed from the bottom of the ship. 'This is a sight worth seeing.'

'What sight is he talking about?' Louis said. 'Hey! Don't leave me alone,' he shouted and Kathy closed the book with a thud and Katie too left the cabin. They all went down the light brown stairs and went over to Ian. They felt like walking in a dream when they walked over to Ian, upon the glass with the cool blue underwater background.

'Amazing sight, isn't it?' Ian said to them while still looking down.

All were awestruck. Never had they seen rather, never had they thought they'll see such a beautiful sight in their lives

'Woah!' exclaimed Mark.

The colorful fishes on top of all made everything look very beautiful. They were in alluring colors like Red and blue, green and white, crimson and purple, yellow and lilac and many more.

'Seems as if they're painted by a wonderful artist,' Kathy spoke up after a great deal of awe striking silence.

Suddenly all the fish raced forward. At the same time they heard footsteps on the stairs.

'Louis must've come,' Katie said, unwilling to budge from the sight.

'Must've got its food guys,' Ian said to the others and all of them waited till the fish were all gone. 'Now let's have ours,' he said standing up finally and with him everyone stood up.

'Showtime over guys,' Kathy said to everyone raising her hands. 'Let's go Fred….. Fred… Hey everyone! Where is Fred?' and she started panicking. All started looking for Fred here and there.

'Louis too is nowhere to be found,' Mark observed suddenly.

'A difficulty on a mountain of difficulties,' Malcolm sighed. 'Keep searching everyone, the last option we have.'

Kathy soon rushed up the brown stairs to see if everything was okay or not and if Fred and Louis were safe or not. After she reached the deck, she rushed inside the cabin where she, Katie and Louis were sitting earlier. There was Louis, munching on some chocolates.

'Hey! What happened? You can't barge in like that,' Louis said, irritated, being disturbed.

Kathy remained gaping, expressionless.

'What's the matter?' Louis asked.

'If you're here, where did Fred go?'

'Fred's lost,' Louis asked.

Kathy nodded. 'I think so. We assumed you to be down there,' she said.

'I never came down,' Louis said casually.

'Then where is Fred?' Kathy screamed and ran back to tell the others what had happened. She was halfway down the stairs when she heard Katie's shrill screaming voice.

'Fred!'

Chapter 10

Rise From Death

Kathy now rushed down faster. The thought process in her mind was all jammed up. Nothing except "What's the matter actually" came to her mind. She was all heated up and so was everyone.

'What's the matter?' she asked shaking Katie furiously by her shoulder.

Katie pointed a trembling finger towards the direction in which a black man was sinking down. He had, for safety reasons, loaded all the ammunition he needed on his body. He was in the scuba diving suit and had on with him an oxygen supply for easy breathing. Suddenly the man wriggled out of the oxygen cylinder, feeling all the weight come on his body. And then was nothing. No oxygen. No breathing. No life. He sank in and in. All was right except for one thing. That man was nearly dying. They saw all this through the glass.

'Fred! Fred!' everyone gasped gesturing him to grab the oxygen cylinder. He waved a "bye" and went down and down until he became a speck and was seen no more.

'How…did…that…happen?' Kathy asked trembling all over.

'We too don't know. We were looking around for him when suddenly we saw him drifting into the picture and then in front of this glass. We' don't know what happened, when he went from here, why he went there or anything,' Malcolm said.

'Maybe Kathy,' Louis said suddenly appearing out of the blue, coming downstairs with his hefty body, 'when you said you heard me coming down it was Fred who went up because I never came down,' and finally saying this he thwacked onto the sofa kept there.

'The only logical explanation we have,' Mark said.

'Because Louis never came downstairs and there is no ghost who would haunt us. And that too when we know Fred had gone upstairs,' Ian said. 'Well done, Louis.'

'My pleasure and he sipped the Coca Cola from the can he had brought downstairs with him.

'Nothing can be done now. The ship is incessantly on the move till we arrive at our destination,' Mark said.

'Actually right,' Ian said. 'No use crying over spilt milk.'

A dark silence pervaded then. No one knowing what to say. Kathy was still in shock and so was Katie, horrified. Kathy owed her life to him for protecting her when the bomb was to explode in her building. After watching the beautiful scene of the underwater with dull and scared eyes for about half an hour, all stood up to leave for upstairs. As they walked up the stairs, they saw it as a path to Fred's death.

After they reached the deck, they all went into their suites. And started packing up, knowing they would reach by evening. Suddenly there were shouts coming from everyone's suites.

'My gun is missing,' shouted Kathy.

'And my bombs too,' Louis shouted.

'My ammunition is also gone,' Ian yelled from another side.

'Oh my!' Malcolm sighed. 'He's taken all our things.'

'Doesn't matter. Think in a different way. While dying, the great man used our things to fight bravely and survive. That includes my oxygen cylinder,' Mark said.

'Hang on Mark. Why did you bring an oxygen cylinder?'

'Because,' Mark said, struggling as to how to tell him the reason, 'I was in constant fright of the ship being drowned. So… you see.'

'Moron,' Malcolm said, annoyingly. 'Why would we drown?'

'Well, I don't know,' Mark said shrugging his shoulders. 'I'm clueless. You ask really hard questions.'

'Eighty one kilometers left,' said the computer.

A man came up from the ship's rear. Dripping wet, he wore a swimming suit ripped at parts, had a strip of bullets, half used and had two guns, one in each hand. He had a grim expression on his face, seemed completely exhausted and weary. He crawled at the start before he stood up and started walking along the deck. He opened the door of the main big suite, feeling so fatigued, that he very powerlessly opened it. He kicked it open, the spotless white door.

Inside he saw six people sitting, one in a brown leather jacket and one in a black leather jacket. Under the jackets they were clad in white. The other four men sat clad wholly in black and had glasses of drinks in their hands. As soon as they saw the man in the swimsuit enter the suite, they were panic stricken. The man was continually looking down.

'It was a great hunch,' he said in a deep voice.

Everyone heaved a sigh of relief.

'Nothing to worry. Fred is dead. It all went as smooth as planned.'

The main two leather jacket people looked at each other and touched their glasses.

'Well done boy, alluring him to his death. We've done our job pretty well. Let's drink to this moment,' the man in the brown jacket said, who seemed to be the leader and everyone raised a toast.

After some minutes, the men saw the man, still standing there with his head looking downwards.

'Hey. You there. Join us. It's a moment to celebrate,' the man in the black jacket said, the assistant.

'I have to still complete my job,' the man in the swimsuit replied.

'And what is that?'

With a reflex the man in the swimsuit took out two machine guns from nowhere and pointed them towards the six people.

'Game over guys. My next job is to terminate you.' he said with a wicked grin.

'Woah! Easy now. We aren't paying you for this,' the leader said.

He just said, 'I know,' and started firing the bullets from the guns furiously. The six people ducked, trying to save themselves from the deadly attack.

'What are you morons doing here. Go and get your guns and kill this traitor,' the assistant yelled at the four men in black.

The four men scurried here and there to find their guns, in vain. They took out their pistols and started banging bullets at the man, hiding from behind the sofas.

'Blow out his brains,' the leader yelled.

The man in the swimsuit somersaulted and released an array of bullets at the first man. Within seconds, the man clad in black was a body.

Three men still continued on to shoot at him. He dodged the bullets and started firing mercilessly at them. A man who was shooting from behind the wooden table succumbed to the bullets.

'Don't let him leave alive,' the leader said.

"Two down. Four to go," the swimmer thought.

The swimmer, while still shooting, started walking backwards and within a fraction of a second, disappeared from the suite.

'Strange man. Here we fire, there goes General Dyer,' one of the shooters said.

'It's no time for lame jokes. Let's go and find him,' the leader said. 'By the way, it sounded like nonsense.'

'Correct. We've got no time to waste,' said the assistant. And they all banged out of the door. The deck was totally empty. They suddenly heard a splash. All went over to look what had happened. They saw a plank of wood floating in the water below.

'He's escaped you fools. We're doomed now,' the leader screamed in rage.

'Maybe he has drowned, sir. It's just the plank that's floating,' the man in black said.

'Maybe he's right,' the assistant said, foolishly.

'He must've jumped in with the plank of wood and then might have been drowned,' the other man in black said, all looking at the same piece wood which was upon discussion.

'I'm not gonna believe till I check it. Anchor the ship right here,' the leader shouted.

One man went in and stopped the ship and came out again.

'Both of you, wear your swimming suits and be ready,' the leader ordered next.

'But why…'

'Just do it. No questions,' said the raged leader.

After fifteen minutes the two men came out of their suites, clad in the heavy swimsuits and oxygen cylinders.

'All of us now in the life boat. You two are going to go deep into the water to find out the man,' said the irritated leader. All of them quietly followed him and sat in the life boat.

As soon as they sat in the life boat.

Bang!

And suddenly from nowhere a bullet ripped and divided the rope of the lifeboat into two. Down it came crashing into the water. The four people screamed loudly. The ship started moving forward with a high speed. The four people in the boat were stuck, right where they fell.

Who fired? From where was the bullet fired? How were we tricked into this? Who did all this? Where was the man? Did he drown or not? Did he die or not? Was he alive? All sorts of questions popped in their minds.

The next second saw a huge fire mass on the place where the boat had been. The ashes mingled with the water.

Chapter 11

The Spitfires

'Fifty eight kilometers left,' beeped the computer.

'Will we make it today,' asked the seasick Louis.

'Be patient,' said Malcolm, dully. 'And perhaps yes, to answer your question.

All were very sad. Fred was the one they had thought of from the minute they saw him die before their eyes. Never did they expect such a thing to happen and that too so suddenly. "How did he die just by diving into the water?" was the question that disturbed everyone's minds. But whatever had happened was very unexpected. The indication seen on everyone's face was just exasperation for taking up this task.

'Forty seven kilometers left,' the computer said after covering some distance.

'Stop the numbers,' an annoyed Ian said.

'As you say sir,' the computer replied.

'They're near. Twenty six kilometers to reach their destination and twenty one to invite their death,' a man said.

'I yield to your words,' said a girl with long blonde hair standing beside the man, who sat in front of a large screen with two smaller screens beside the larger screen. One showed the radar and the other one showed their den.

The couple was not seen very properly. They were just the silhouettes of a man and a lady talking to each other. The man sipped the fuming something from the cup and placed it on the large table consisting of the controls. A very wide variety of controls that were complicated than love.

'It is around a quarter to five now. We have to wait for an hour. Quarter to six and the game is over,' he said with a wicked grin.

'I follow your orders. I will be ready at the precise time,' the girl said. 'I know all the plans too, don't I?' she smiled and walked off.

The man saw her walk off and when she couldn't be seen anymore, he turned towards the screens again.

'Come my colleagues. You're welcome. You give me yourself, I will show you myself. Follow my map, fall into my trap, before you head for the gap, you'll turn into scrap,' saying this he exploded into a chill of laughter. 'And then I'll get the genuine map.'

And he exploded a chill of cold laughter again in the silence of the place.

'I'll achieve my aim at last,' he thought, being happy.

He checked the watch. Four fifty five it showed. Fifty minutes to count.

'Victory!' he bellowed, not being able to control the euphoria.

'I am quitting Fitz,' Katie said. 'Don't try to convince and drag me into this. I'm not going to suffer any longer.'

'Is that it? The reason for why you're quitting?' Ian counter questioned.

'Not just her Fitz. Me too,' Malcolm spoke up, with his usual cold voice.

'You too? But why? What exactly is that matter?' Ian asked annoyingly.

'He's right. You can't quit at least at this time,' Kathy too tried to convince them.

'Can I know what has happened? Or shall I continue on my own?' Ian said now angrily.

'Do you think you can continue on your own?' Katie asked with sarcasm.

'Well…' he fell in doubt. 'No,' he said then. 'But what has happened, you need to say.'

'Well. I gave you my reason,' Katie said.

'Great. I need Malcolm's reason now,' Ian said.

'Hear it then. Do you know where Mark is?' Malcolm questioned.

'No,' Ian said. 'Must be up in his cabin.'

'Not there.'

Ian breathed heavily and said, 'Impossible. That guy never comes out of his cabin often.'

'I'm positive he's not there.'

'You sure you checked his cabin and not someone else's?'

'I'm pretty sure,' was the strong reply from Malcolm.

After a moment of silence Ian spoke up.

'In the basement?'

'No.'

In the pool?'

'No.'

'Somewhere on the deck?'

'Nowhere on the ship,' replied Malcolm.

'What?' gaped Fitz. 'Mark too has disappeared?'

'That's what is troubling me. The disappearance of Fred first and now it's Mark. I can't take this any longer.'

'He seriously has a point for quitting Fitz,' Kathy whispered in Fitz's ears. 'It actually leaves on just we five. I, you, him, Katie and that fatty.'

'Hmm. I see,' Ian said after a great deal of thinking.

'It seems to me a very dangerous task now. I'm afraid our lives now,' Malcolm said, a bit terrified.

'I think Mark is playing a game with us,' Ian said then. 'His things are there in his cabin?'

'Yes.'

'I'm sure then. He's playing a game. Let him be concealed. How long will he hide? We ought to continue on our work. But please don't quit friends,' Ian said humbly.

Silence pervaded for some time. After a long interval, the silence was broken by Katie.

'Seeing Fitz's humble and gentle request, I've made up my mind to stay,' she said, smiling.

'Even I've made up my mind,' Malcolm said and stopped for a few seconds.

'What is the decision?' Ian asked curiously.

'Bring the bazookas from the ammunition room,' he told Fitz.

'What?' Ian said in surprise and a little puzzled.

'Do as I say,' he said in the same cold voice.

Ian rushed off to get two bazookas.

'What is the distance left?' Malcolm asked to the computer.

'You told me stop the numbers,' the computer replied instantly.

'Well now you can,' Malcolm said.

'Stupid machine,' Louis said.

Ian soon returned with two of them.

'Seven kilometers left,' the computer beeped.

'We're nearing the point now. Danger will come anytime now,' Malcolm warned in his calm voice.

'What point? What danger?' a puzzled Kathy asked.

'Never mind that,' Malcolm said slapping Fitz's back. 'Just pay attention.'

'What is he saying?' Ian whispered to Katie. She shrugged her shoulders.

'Let's go on the deck now.' Ian followed his lead.

'He's got mad I think,' Katie said to Kathy.

After they reached the front of the ship, Malcolm looked around as if searching something.

'Great. Great scene. Out of danger, for present,' he said taking a bazooka from Fitz.

'What is all this about?' Ian kept on asking repeatedly but the calm Malcolm remained quiet.

'Six kilometers left,' the computer beeped from inside loud enough for them to hear. Louis was still there in bed.

'Great. We're nearing the danger zone,' Malcolm kept on saying.

'For what are we standing here? I'm asking this for the last time,' Ian asked Malcolm furiously.

'You'll get the answer soon enough,' Malcolm said.

Ian was losing patience now. He was fuming at Malcolm's every sentence now which he thought to be non-sensual.

Just then the two girls came out on the deck.

'Anything in for us?' Katie asked.

'You would like not like to be in this place now,' Malcolm said.

'Why?'

'Because danger is approaching. Rather, we're approaching danger,' he said with a grave voice.

'Right,' Ian said looking angrily at Malcolm who was more heighted than him. 'Get inside.'

'No way we're going in when you're out,' Kathy said, shaking her head sideways.

The boys tried much to convince them but the girls were adamant.

And suddenly the computer said something which pricked Malcolm's ears.

'Five kilometers left.'

'It's five forty five now. Give the orders for launch,' the man said, his whole attention on the big screen in anticipation of what was to happen next.

'Yes,' the girl said and pressed a red button spoke in front of the mic.

'Path clear. The Jets are ordered to be launched right now. Over.'

'We're ready. Over,' came the reply.

'Done,' the girl said to the man.

'Good,' all his attention still on the screen.

A few seconds later, there was a rumbling sound of a motor starting. A booming engine start.

'Wait in curiosity,' he started telling to the girl and signaled her to sit on the chair beside him on the chair. 'My rivals from eternity are going to depart their lives in front of my eyes. I will get what I want. I will be the master of my life. There will be on one to catch me. No police, no FBI, and no one will know about anything. This is the moment. I want to live it,' he said, his teeth clenched.

'It is quarter to six,' he shouted triumphantly.

'It's five kilometers left. Anytime now,' Malcolm said.

Ian was still mad at him for not telling the reason. Ian was thinking that had lunacy entered Malcolm or what? What had happened to him? What was going on? What was the danger? He was lost in thoughts very soon.

'Ian you okay?' Malcolm asked him, shaking his shoulder. He moved as if woken up from a dream.

'Hmm. Yes,' he said, scowling at Malcolm.

Suddenly, a roaring sound caught their attention. They saw two aircrafts come out of the hedges. Green and off-white in color.

They were seen coming closer and closer.

'Someone must have come for a picnic,' Ian said, not knowing what exactly to say.

'Stupid logic. No one comes with a jet on a picnic,' Malcolm replied instantly.

As the planes came nearer Malcolm asked Katie to fetch the binoculars kept on the table of his suite. Katie did as told. He then saw at the planes through the binoculars. After five minutes or so he said,

'This is it,' and took the binoculars off. 'Be ready Fitz. It's going to be a great game.'

Saying this he aimed the bazooka at the nearing plane and advised Into do the same. Ian hesitated a bit but then reluctantly pointed his bazooka in the plane's direction.

As they planes neared and were just a few meters away from them, they saw a big "V19" written on one jet and a big "V10" written on the other.

'I'm not doing it,' Ian suddenly gave up and threw down the bazooka.

'You have to,' Malcolm screamed against the booming voice of the planes. At the same time Louis came out.

'Hey! That's the sound of the 1940s spitfire. A dangerous jet used by the British RAf in the Second World War. It has automatic guns and stuff,' he said and looked up to the spitfires coming closer.

'No Malcolm. I'm not doing it.'

'What's the matter?' Malcolm asked.

'I'm kind of scared,' he said.

'Come what may, I have to save everyone on board,' thought Malcolm and with this thought in mind, he aimed at plane with V10 written on it.

He started the countdown in his mind.

Three, Two, One, Shoot!

And up went the bazooka, flying at such a great speed, it could rip off a car into two if it wouldn't be explosive. It went high into the air and crashed into the desired jet.

Ian turned to look a very big fire mass in the air, on the place where the jet had been with a loud explosion voice. A gust of air blew from the explosion, causing their hair to be ruffled.

Malcolm looked towards Ian and grinned. 'How was the shot,' he meant to say.

Instead he said, 'Are you going to shoot the second one or not? Or shall I borrow your bazooka?'

'Well, I don't know,' Ian replied picking up his bazooka. 'I'll try.'

And Ian aimed at the remaining plane. As soon as he was going to shoot, the bazooka went out of balance and Ian was falling. Katie and Kathy rushed over to him and held him on his hands, on either sides. Ian ran to take charge of the bazooka. Ian was nearly fainting. Malcolm couldn't take this anymore. He fired an angry look at the V19 and picked up Fitz's bazooka. He aimed for the jet.

There crashed the bazooka in the plane.

The next moment saw an orange fireball in the sky with some air exerted out and black parts and ashes falling out from the orange ball, and submerging into the water.

'No.'

A shrill scream echoed from between the hills.

'Impossible,' the man said out of breath, almost panicking. 'How did this happen? How were these idiots prepared for the event? How did they know about this?' he bellowed. 'You saw that right,' he said turning towards the girl now.

'Yes.'

'What conclusion can be drawn then?' he said banging his hand on the table.

'They knew about it already. That's all I can infer about it,' she said, sipping from a can of Coca Cola.

'Exactly what I think. Please review the footage and draw out all information you can, of this incident. Keep tracking them.'

'Yes,' and she turned back and vanished again.

'An accidental coincidence or a readied attack?' the man wondered and with a thud, sunk into the chair.

'Three kilometers to go,' the computer beeped.

'Nearing our destination at last,' Louis said jumping out of bed.

'Take care fatty. You'll get hurt,' Kathy said, still shocked about what had happened outside in the deck. Kathy and Katie had rushed in soon after the firing had started. They had seen everything through the glass pane. Scared girls.

Then gradually Malcolm and Ian entered the suite, with empty barrels.

'We're nearing the shore,' Malcolm said, walking over to the kitchen part. He picked up a sandwich and passed Ian one. Ian asked for Malcolm's sandwich too. Malcolm passed it. Ian heated them in a microwave and then passed one sandwich to Malcolm again.

'Thanks buddy for heating it up,' Malcolm said and started devouring the sandwich while he sat with a thud on the couch. Ian joined him.

'Care for some juice?' Katie asked.

'Yes,' both said simultaneously.

Katie filled two glasses of juice and passed the glasses to them. She gave a final look at Fitz's face hysteria and said,

'I know what it feels like Fitz.'

'What do you mean?' he asked back, puzzled again.

'Curiosity,' she said.

'Elaborate yourself please.'

'Firstly we are followed by a strange white helicopter and then we are saved from being devoured by a shark. We are then saved from not one but three underwater bombs. And then the incident at the Tate Modern. Then the death of Fred and the disappearance of Mark. And then here these jets come to attack us. It all seems horrendous.'

'Indeed,' replied Louis.

'Tow kilometers left,' the computer said.

'All the supplies to be kept on the ship and all the essential materials with to be with us in a backpack, an extra rucksack to be carried, a bedroll would be needed and some snacks. For each one of us,' Kathy said.

'I'm done my eating stuff,' Malcolm said rising from the couch.

'Me too,' said Fitz. 'Louis let's get back to work. You go steer the ship and park it at the right place.'

Everyone set to work, packing their things to be taken on the island. The ship suddenly was steered right extremely violently by Louis. All lost balance for a moment. The ship finally hit the shore.

In the next few minutes, all were ready with their things. With an air of finality and triumph, all of them descended the stairs of the ship, onto the island. Great adventures waited for them. Great mysteries still lay in path for them to be solved. A life full of feats and puzzles waited for them. It was six in the evening.

Chapter 12

The Lion Explodes

'Follow them.'

The island on which they had landed upon was not very big but big enough to house very great hills. The island contained just green bushes and trees and hedges. It was a very cozy and a cold island. The glistening fireflies moved around the bushes, lightening up the leaves and flowers. The moon had started to rise. The isolated island looked as if it had waited for years and years to have guests. The sky was blackening and the stars had started to reveal themselves and their glowing form. Distinctly viewing the future, the North Star was shining bright, to help the great people fulfill their aim. The night was simple.

The shore of the island offered a great place to camp around. It was a semi circular shaped beach with soft sand containing the footsteps of five people all the way from a ship which was anchored on the glossy shore. The beach was a sign of intellectuality. SO beautiful it was, that no one could take eyes off it. Coming to the conclusion, it was just one word that everyone said. spoke. "Marvelous," stretching each syllable.

The ship had already reached the shore. Where to camp? It was the question. Here and there when looked, it seemed all dangerous to camp out there on the shore. It was thought that the cozy cabins would be the most appropriate places to spend the night. And thus was finalized. With a danger waiting.

'We don't have any power here,' Louis said suddenly, fidgeting with the torchlight they had brought with them.

'Power?' Kathy questioned. 'Magnetic, electric, which power?'

'I'm sure you won't use magnetic power in conditions where you've no electricity,' Louis answered, slackening his eyelids.

'Actually Louis is right,' Malcolm said. 'Torch lights provide the best option in these conditions,' and he grabbed the torch from Louis' hand.

'So?' Ian said, a bit nervously.

'So?' the girls replied with the same look and then giggled.

Ian turned towards Malcolm and Louis. As he opened his mouth to say something, it was Malcolm who spoke in a whisper.

'If you are going to tell that "why do they giggle on small things?" I have no answer to that,' he said while searching for the batteries to be put in the torches, theirs and the girls'.

'Here they are Malcolm,' Louis said giving the batteries to Malcolm he had found in his bag.

Malcolm snatched the batteries with a look of disgust. After the batteries were put Louis grabbed the torches from Malcolm's hands and flashed them on, directly in Malcolm's eyes.

'Stop that Louis,' Malcolm said, irritated. 'At least not in my eyes!'

'Will two torches be suff… Ouch! Louis! Can you stop that stupid thing please,' Ian said, annoyingly.

'Well, that's the way I fell when you call me fatso,' Louis grumbled.

'We'll stop it if you stop this thing right now,' an irritated Malcolm spoke.

'Okay. But remember your promise,' Louis said, putting away the torches.

'SO, I was speaking of the torches. Maybe we'll want one more,' Ian said and continued his discourse on the disadvantages of taking just two torches with them, for the next twenty minutes. All of them had started yawning and felt pretty bored and tired.

'I'm out of this Ian. Good night,' Kathy said and wrapped the blanket around her as swiftly as she could and slept.

'Good night Ian,' said everyone and jumped to bed.

'Oh! No one's listening,' Ian mumbled and he too went to bed, no option left.

Up above them the bright moon shone upon the far stretches of green on the island. The green bushes and hedges and the great trees had so densely covered themselves as to form a canopy of green with the bright silver moonlight upon it. The sea waves lashed upon the shore while the moonlight spread its influence over the night. The five friends were sleeping soundly, unaware of the island, the dangers it would cause and the future.

While on one side, the fatigued five were in bed, on the other side a black figure upon their ship, held something in its hand. IT whispered loudly into the cold island air. 'Victory.'

The five friends soundly slept in their tent.

'Is everyone ready?' Louis called out.

'Yes,' Ian and Malcolm replied at once. Kathy and Katie were nowhere around them.

'Where are the girls,' Louis asked.

'Well, they've gone to the ship to pack some food supplies for today, especially for you,' Ian said with a grin.

'Why me?'

'Because you gulp so much,' Malcolm said.

'I don't. Actually I just can drink three cans of Coke, eat two whole large sized plates of salad and four pizzas at one go,' Louis said, water trickling out of his mouth.

'Speaking of Coke, I forgot my carton in the ship itself. Ian please hold on my bag for a second,' and pushing his bag in Ian's hand which they had packed early in the morning. Each one had their own bags with them.

'Good day, ladies,' Malcolm said, he entering the ship and the girls exiting the ship simultaneously.

'Yeah,' they said, climbing down the stairs.

Fifteen minutes elapsed. The four people were waiting for Malcolm outside their camp.

'Malcolm,' Louis bellowed in his sturdy voice. The other three stuck their fingers in their ears.

'I can't find my cans,' he replied back. They could see his figure moving inside the meeting room distinctly.

'They're not there in the meeting room,' Kathy shouted back. 'The cans are in Fred's room.'

But despite of her telling that the cans weren't there, for about another five minutes, Malcolm stayed in the meeting room and then went out of it. After ten minutes he came out with six cans between ten fingers.

'Something is fishy,' Katie whispered to Ian and Kathy.

'We'll see,' Ian replied.

Seeing the four friends waiting for him from the past half an hour, he rushed over to them.

'I'm done now. Let's move,' Malcolm said huffing.

Louis scowled at him but at that time it didn't matter much to Malcolm.

'Okay then. Right into the bushes,' Ian ordered.

They put forth their footsteps towards achieving their goal, with dangers and risks in. They had walked for just five hundred meters in the hedges and then were in open ground. They stopped dead in their tracks. They saw a herculean yellow paw sticking out from behind a bush. A loud growl and the rummaging of the dead leaves on the ground followed. The roar then shook their insides. It seemed as if it lied in their wait.

A danger waited.

Nothing was well.

'All ready again, to die, my friends. Now this one is going to be my second trick for your afterlife,' the man said with a tinge of happiness and a bulk of anger, all mixed up. He was still seated in front of the large screen, sipping his coffee. He was satisfied today.

'Why so happy today?' the girl suddenly came in the den, emerging from the bushes.

'Well, it's a secret but you ought to know it.'

'Hmm.'

'The matter is that I've...'

All was well, with him.

Very soon, the owner of the paw emerged from the bush. Slowly, the yellowness of it began to spread, its face emerging first while the body followed. It had a great golden mane and shiny eyes speaking of its predators. The yellow body was just too good to hide itself for its hunting.

Within three meters of the place where they stood, there stood a mighty lion, getting ready to pound upon its feast, the human flesh, of five tasty humans, looking at them boldly, directly in the eye. It was a great day for him.

'Go on, my friend. As fast as you can. Finish them off. Today's your day,' the man said suddenly turning over to the screen, cutting off the connection between him and the girl.

'Ready to die?' Louis whispered in Ian's ears.

'Not so soon,' Ian said and took out his gun and aimed directly at the lion's face.

'No Ian. Don't do this,' Malcolm said sticking out his hand in front of Ian.

'It's ready to pound,' Katie said. 'Back off Ian, please,' she urged.

But those words weren't strong enough to affect Ian. With a heavy heart and filled with grief, he got ready to pull the trigger. The other four hearts grieved with a sudden pain of detachment from their friends. They were going to be separated for life. They would never meet each other. Their quest would remain unfinished. It was both, a dangerous and a sorrowful moment for them.

'I'm going to pull the trigger on the count of three,' Ian finally declared.

All moved a little, with fright and nervousness.

'Three.'

The lion shrugged his shoulders to get ready for the attack.

'Two.'

The lion started running. All stood with their hearts in their mouth.

'One.'

The lion leapt up and Ian, not knowing what to do, pulled the trigger.

Bang!

The bullet sped directly in the lion's mouth. The next moment they knew, they were alive and a huge fire mass had been there where the lion was in mid air.

All gaped in astonishment. What was the matter? Surely a bullet would not explode a lion. But this so called lion had erupted into flames. How was this possible? Was it a dream or was it a reality? Was that really a lion? Who was playing these tricks with them? Who was behind all this?

They next thing heard were the footsteps of something, making a crunching sound on the dead, dry leaves. As the sound neared, the silhouette of the object was seen. It wasn't an object. It was a man. He seemed young, with a bazooka in one hand and the other hand's fist clenched. Due to the widespread fog on the island, he could not be seen properly. As he came more nearer, his glossy blue eyes made everything evident. His face was turning out to be visible. He became the reason to send a chill down the spine of the five friends. It was a miracle. The dream-reality dilemma was further strengthened. They knew this man. He was the one they could not stop thinking of from the past 24 hours. All were brimmed up with excitement and amazement at the same time.

All cried in one voice.

'Fred!'

Chapter 13

A Lone Warrior

'Freeze,' Ian suddenly said, pointing his gun at the man. The man stopped. 'Prove yourself.'

'That I'm Fred, right Ian?' the man said, with a sly smile. 'There stand Kathy, Katie, Louis the fatso and Malcolm.'

'He knows our names Ian. Set down your gun,' Kathy said.

'No. I don't believe him. Already many disasters have taken place. I don't want another one,' Ian said perspiring all over.

'I didn't that day Ian,' the man said, and slowly took footsteps towards them. Ian backed one step off with every advancing footstep of the man, maintain the distance.

'Are you out of mind?' Malcolm said in a raised voice.

'No I'm not,' Ian replied in a voice higher than Malcolm.

'We stole the Kohinoor together. Then we went to the Tate where we were followed by a man and then from him we received and map of this very "Au" Island. I stopped by in your room after the Kohinoor robbery and I had told you something. Now do you believe me?' the man said and spread his arms.

Everyone except Ian ran and hugged him at once. All were very happy. Big smiles flooded over their faces. Ian was still standing there, his mouth opened. He was astounded.

'Still shocked?' Fred said and went over to him and hugged him.

Ian did not know how to respond. He was so shocked he never closed his mouth.

'How did you come out alive,' Kathy asked.

'I'll tell everything.'

'Now Fred, tell us what had happened with you,' Katie said.

'You want to hear it now?' Fred questioned, puzzled.

'Now of course. You die and suddenly come out alive and that too right here in front of us. That surely requires an explanation,' Malcolm said.

'I will provide an explanation. But while walking. I want to show you something. Listen to my narrative,' said Fred and started.

All started walking. Ian walked behind the group.

'That day when we were seeing the fishes, they were so beautiful. Red and blue, black and grey, crimson and yellow and lilac and purple ones. They seemed very adorable to everyone of us and me too but just for a second. I used Louis' rather Holmes' method of observing things. If you all remember, the blue fish suddenly raced forward. I curiously looked at it. I saw light reflecting from its body and a nut glistening. At that time I was sure that this was a hunch. I wanted to investigate. I was curious. So I ran up and got into the scuba suit and took some ammunition and plunged into the sea. And one more thing, I'm sorry for taking your things. I apologize. I took them because I was in a hurry and I couldn't find my things. I think I haven't brought them in the first place. All of that later.

'As I dived into the water, I slipped and got hurt on the chin. After getting underwater, I tried to go down and turned to see if everything was okay or not. I tried to see you all through the glass but what I saw was that you were panicking to find me and you thought the fish raced forward. But in real, when I saw below the ship, the fish were there, stuck below it. The most amazing thing was that they were glimmering with red lights. Fishes with glimmering red lights. I was shocked and instantly sensed that they were robotic bombs.'

'I swam up from the place I was and up at the ship's bottom. I then started dethatching them with bare hands. I was uprooting bombs with bare hands. I don't understand from where did that power come? I uprooted all of them and sent them deep down into the sea with the help of the magnet I carried with me. I attracted all the fishes to the magnet and then flushed the magnet deep down with all my might.'

'I smiled at my work but just then something pricked me on my right leg. It was paining intensely from the moment it pricked. I could no longer swim on my own. All that power in me was lost. I was feeling feeble and weak. The whole ship passed over me, while I remained stranded on that stop. When the glass came over me, I started drowning. I saw your faces peering down at me in horror but there was nothing I could do. I was powerless. You all kept on looking at me till I couldn't see you. And that was my end, I had thought.'

'But I was wrong. Very wrong. When I was at considerable depth, I saw a yellow light heading towards my direction. It directly flashed in my eye so I was unable to make out what was it? As it neared, I figured it out to be a mini submarine. The same mini submarine which was launched by Howard Nile three months ago. The submarine came to where I was and robotic arms came out of the sides of the submarine and grabbed me like a doll. The submarine's entrance opened. The arms put me there inside and returned to their positions.'

'The inside of that submarine was huge. It was like the Harry Potter tent. Small from the outside, great on the inside. I tried to walk but my feet won't comply. I was sitting there on the ground. Below me was a Persian rug, one of the best, red in color. It was a very well equipped space, seemed more like a living room. Pictures of cats and dogs painted on oval dishes decorated the wall. The red sofa sets added the splendor. The glass tables further were very beautiful. The white was the best match against the red objects. And then on the farther end of the living room was a big computer with a large screen in front of it and some controls below. Some papers and red pencils too were present. On the screen, the path in which the submarine went was being shown.'

'While I was observing everything around and thinking if I was the only one in this great submarine, a man clad in black from top to bottom appeared. He wore a dull expression on his face. He emerged out of a room and went and sat on the chair kept in front of the computer, his back towards me. I was wondering who on earth was he? Slowly, sipping his coffee he turned around.'

'"Welcome Fred," he said. "Welcome Fred, to your death."'

'As soon as he said that, I felt my blood boiling. How can one lure me to my death so easily? I thought.'

'"That didn't rhyme even a bit," I said becoming bold. I was feeling my strength return back to me.'

'"Doesn't matter, does it?" he replied back.'

'"And you're sent here for?" I asked.'

'"Your killing. You're the…"'

'"And by?" I cut him off.'

'"I won't tell you that," he shot back.'

'Suddenly, the next moment he pounded on me. Recalling my reflexes, I swiftly moved out of the way. He landed on his nose, and it started bleeding really hard. He held his nose and wailed loudly. Seeking that chance, I kicked him once more on his nose, now able enough to walk on myself.'

'And surprisingly, he became unconscious in just one kick. I left him as he was, nose bleeding and the rug redder. I went towards the computer, curious as to what was in there and what lay out there. I then saw some papers on the controls. I picked up one of it. Useless as it was, I discarded it. There was one more paper below it. On it were scribbled some lines and some places, all in red pencil. As I was trying to figure it out, the corner of my right eye caught a red light blinking. I turned my head towards my right. I saw radar with a red dot blinking on it. I, at first, assumed it to be the position of the submarine.'

'"It is not what you think," the man spoke, getting up on his legs, his nose still bleeding. He was still feeling dizzy I suppose, because he wasn't standing straight. And then, within a fraction of a second he pulled out a sword out of the show piece shield hanging on the wall. It was actually a fencing sword. I somersaulted and grabbed the remaining one, not to be left out. And our swordplay started.'

'I got wounded, I bruised him, but I was the dominating one. I cleared him out after a long fight, with a blow directly in his arm. He fell down lifeless. I forgot to ask his name, though. Then finally I kicked him on his stomach in hatred. And then I went to the controls. I concentrated hard on what the man had said. I did my analysis and concluded that the blinking red dot on the radar was not of the submarine in which I was. It was the position of a ship. Very different from ours. I switched on the computer controls.

'"Where to, sir?" the computer asked.'

'"In the direction of the ship on the radar," I said with a wide grin.'

And the submarine sped like a car.

'Well,' that's a long story. 'Do you have more to tell?' Louis asked as Fred paused .

'A lot more to tell my friend,' Fred replied.

'Then go on,' Ian said. 'The story is becoming awesome. Go ahead.'

'I don't think I need to go ahead. The rest of the story will be published in the newspaper all by itself, won't it Malcolm?' Fred said and winked to Malcolm.

'Oh, right,' the newspaper fanatic Malcolm said.

'By then, let me tell you another story I read in the submarine while traveling in the direction of the ship. It is a great one,' Fred said.

'Oh! You had a book in there,' Ian said.

'Yes,' Fred replied. 'So, all ready to hear the story?'

'Yes,' everyone said at once.

Chapter 14

Tunnel Problem

'That was a pretty good story,' Louis said after Fred had completed the story.

'A really unexceptional one,' Katie said, awestruck.

'I'm speechless,' Malcolm said, his mouth still open.

'A brave man indeed, whoever it was,' Kathy said.

'I mainly focused on the moves of the man. Really very striking,' Ian said after a great deal of astonishing silence.

'Thanks,' Fred said, 'and sorry once again to take your things without permission,' Fred said, letting a little smile. 'I was in a great hurry and you know the curiousness of my love of investigating.' His healthy body was covered under an olive green shirt with half folded sleeves. And on top of that he wore a sleeveless coat. Black jeans covered his legs and the black shoes added splendor to his looks. With the bazooka still in his hand, he got up from the rocks they all were sitting on.

The banks of the island were still seen. Far away a thick fog took up, some distance away from the island. It was all misty there. The lush green leaves of the vegetation there were losing its luster gradually. The sunlight had started dimming thought it was just around 11 in the morning. A cool breeze started blowing. The sky was overcast.

'Seems it's going to rain,' Ian said looking up.

'Actually it won't,' Malcolm said. 'I've read many books related to islands and have always figured out this climate to be the actual climate of the island. Grey sky, misty air, foggy surrounding and dull atmosphere.'

'Right, actually,' said Louis getting up. They all could see the waves lash upon the shore but no signs of drizzling were seen.

'You have great presence of mind Fred,' Kathy said at last after a long silence due to everyone engrossed in watching the sight around them. The breeze was becoming gentler and at the same time stronger. 'You be like Sherlock Holmes.

'She's right. You notice very minutely,' Katie said. 'Like the fishes and the nuts upon them and everything.'

'I'll take that as a compliment. Thanks. But that's a specialty I found in myself due to Louis. He was the one who deduced and brought us to this place and I was inspired by him. So I noticed the fishes and had an adventure and here I am,' Fred said, playing with his fingers. He looked towards the now grey-turned sea. The barks of the trees turned damp and the atmosphere turned mild.

'So, what was with you guys? Had fun?' he asked at last.

'We shot down just two spitfires,' Katie said smiling and winking at Ian.

'The jet spitfire?'

'Yes,' replied Kathy.

'Hold on. It was the boys, precisely Malcolm and Ian who shot down the jets,' Katie said. Fred opened his mouth wide.

'Malcolm, you too shot down a plane,' he asked.

'What do you mean? I did,' Malcolm replied with troubled hysteria.

'And yes, one more thing to tell. Mark has disappeared,' Louis said.

'That's the second dreadful thing I've heard,' Fred said.

'Well, what was the first?'

'Malcolm shot down a spitfire,' and they all burst into laughter, save Malcolm.

'I apologize. I was kidding. So, how exactly did he disappear?'

'We haven't got any single hint of it,' Ian said. 'Malcolm wanted to talk to him and he went to Mark's suite but he wasn't there. Malcolm searched for him on the entire ship but he was nowhere to be found.'

Just then something caught their attention. A bird fluttered by, red in color with blue wings and a yellow tail. It sat on the tree just opposite to them.

'That is the most uncommon bird I've ever seen,' Kathy said. 'It's so beautiful.'

'But according to whatever little I know about birds, I can say that it is the most uncommon of a bird to fly by in this weather.' Everyone turned their heads. It was Malcolm, the businessman who had spoken.

'Don't look at me like that,' he scowled.

'Yeah. Actually I'm right,' he said after sometime with a grin and then suddenly changed his expression to the angry detective look and within the fraction of a second took out his gun and aimed it directly at the bird and shot it. The bird fell down miserably.

All heads turned towards Malcolm now.

'Why did you do that?' Kathy yelled. The others too were furious. They looked on at the plight of the bird.

'It was such a beautiful one. You don't get to see these in the city,' Louis said.

And then everyone simultaneously started yelling at him.

'Wait,' Malcolm shouted, his voice overpowering the others'. 'Can you hear that voice?'

Everyone quietned. The sound of some short circuit taking place in wires was distinctly heard.

'Where's that sound coming from?' the only question that ran in everybody's mind.

'There. Look at that bird,' said Fred pointing at the bird. For a few seconds the blue sparks continuously jumped out of the bird from the spot where the bullet had been shot. The next moment, the bird went up in flames and the parts of the bird separated. The metal rings and the loops and the battery and the motor and everything started popping out of the fire at last a black object popped out. Fred picked it up. He observed it closely. And he kept it in his pocket.

'Never mind that,' Fred said.

'Why did you do that?' Ian yelled. 'It was such a beautiful bird.'

'I did just what I had to,' Malcolm calmly replied. Fred started clapping his hands, very suddenly.

'I really do appreciate your thinking Malcolm,' he said. 'I really do. Now let me tell you further that…' But Kathy, Katie, Ian and Louis weren't listening, still dumbstruck.

How could a bird contain such mechanical parts?

'You think right my friends,' said the man on his usual place in his usual den, right in front of the screen.

'You escaped this time Fred, but the next time your dead body will glorify my pride. It is a pity that their thinking restricts them only to their so called adventures and not the reasons behind them. Though my Bird-Camera has been destroyed, I don't care,' he seemed to talk to himself. 'What I possess is,' and he turned around his seat to see into the shine of what he had with him.

'Gold,' he shouted in excitement and ecstasy.

'You see that fog surging up there?' Fred asked everyone, pointing in the direction of the fog. Everyone nodded.

'Well then, that place is a good 7 km away from here,' he said and stopped.

'What's the point?' Kathy asked.

'I want all of you to accompany me there.'

'Why? What's there?' asked Louis, trying to rise high to see the fog.

'It's supposed to remain suspense,' Fred answered grinning.

'Are we going to walk all that distance?!' Louis questioned with a tensed look.

'No my friend. Absolutely not. We aren't going to walk a whole damn 7 km,' Fred said, soothing him.

After about forty five minutes, the ships started. Ian, Kathy Katie and Louis, all four in their ship, the "719". While Malcolm and Fred in another ship, the "M.Cryptic".

'Wait for me till I bring my ship next to yours,' Fred told Louis and rushed back to the driver's cabin.

'So let's start,' Louis said and with a final sign of the blowing of the ship horns, the two ships left the island.

After fifteen minutes, both the ships hit the shore of somewhere, after passing through the thick white fog. The ships abruptly stopped. All rushed onto the decks to see where they had stopped. The place was another island with far stretches of greenery prevailing upon it, and yet another fog which they had to pass. They started feeling cold now.

'Where are we?' Ian said, feeling nervous. Everyone by now had come down with the supplies needed.

'Where's the map?' Fred asked for it, holding out his open palm. Malcolm rummaged in his bag and then produced the map, and handed it over to Fred.

'Thanks Malcolm,' Fred said and taking the paper he announced, 'We are on, the "Au" Island.'

Everyone developed a puzzled expression. 'What was that island then? Were we tricked? What is going on?' All these questions raced in everyone's mind.

'All your answers later. I think we now ought to find where the gold is exactly located. But before that, I would like to open up the suspense,' Fred said, reading everyone's minds. And saying that, he gestured everyone to follow him. Everyone did as he said.

After about ten minutes of walking, they came to a damp place. An open ground covered with trees on the perimeter. And out of the trees there emerged the figure of a girl. Average in height, fair complexioned and blonde hair. She wore a black hat and black goggles and a completely white outfit. She came towards these six friends. All eyes were on her.

'Who's that?' Louis whispered to Malcolm.

'How do I know?' Malcolm replied loudly.

She slowly advanced towards and group and minutes, there she was, holding her large brown purse.

'You're not...!' exclaimed Ian, gaping at her.

'Emma,' said the girl and took of her glasses. Everyone's faces lit up. After all, a friend not met from a long time came back.

'Where did you find her Fred?' Katie asked, still not believing their childhood friend was in front of them.

'Let me tell you,' Malcolm said with a grin. 'When Fred and I were on our way to the ship to come here, we saw her alone and miserable on the sea banks. On further inquiry, we came to know that she was here with her friends on a holiday, but her friends by mistake left her behind. Then we found her and got her ready. When we came out of the ship, she raced here before us in a way not to be seen and now here she is.'

'We'll ask what happened with her in all these years in detail, afterwards. First, let us complete our mission,' Fred said.

Ian pointed out to Emma.

'Oh! That's no problem. We've already told her everything. She's a part of our plan now,' Fred said, guessing Ian's anxiousness. 'So,' he said opening the map, 'this thing says that the gold lies 2 km from here and the entrance is 400 meters away. Head in that direction company.' And Fred led the way.

All walked on and on for 400 meters straight. They at last reached the spot shown on the map. There were vines and wet mud and much more in between. They passed it all and reached here. And what they saw was two large holes side by side dug out of the mud of the huge hill that stood above them. They seemed like tunnels for their achievement.

'This probably is the entrance,' Ian said, looking at the two wide holes.

'But which one has to be entered?' Fred questioned, puzzled.

'Let's try the left one.' It was Louis who spoke. The group's Sherlock Holmes.

He might be right. And thinking that, without a question, all like ants entered the left hole. It indeed was a tunnel.

'Can anyone imagine this rotten entrance is the way to one of the most expensive things in the world? Hey! My voice is booming,' Malcolm said.

'I think so,' Emma answered Louis.

It was a 1.6 km route to their ultimate destination. They all walked and walked. Everyone was perspiring and couldn't breathe properly due to air insufficiency. As for the visibility, Ian, Katie and Louis all had their torches switched on. After a long and a weary walk they saw the overcast skylight at a distance on the right side of the tunnel.

'Almost there,' Fred said who was leading the way.

Their walk was coming to an end. No one had thought it would be this easy to reach their goal. Then again they landed upon a dilemma. There were tow two exits in front of them.

'Which one to take now Homes? Both the holes at the entrance in the start lead to the same tunnel. Where to now?' Fred shouted loud enough for Louis to hear.

'Let's try the right one first,' Louis yelled from the other part of tunnel. All went in that direction. Louis really wanted to see where it leaded to.

All had made up their minds to re-enter the tunnel and go to the first one if this didn't turn out to have anything.

And the tunnel lead them into the open air. There they stood on the rocks on a high elevation. They glorified what they saw. It was greenery all around. They almost stood150 meters above the ground. They were beneath the open sky and below them were beautiful flowers springing out of the bushes, from the stillness and the solemn voice of nature. Moreover they were overwhelmed that they could now breathe easily. One fall and they could die, that was the height they stood at. They had entered the second tunnel to adore the nature and nothing else. Nothing was in front of them. No glass, no wall, just the far stretches of green of the island and great hills.

'Where are we?' Ian asked, almost unconsciously clutching on to Louis, while he looked down from the place they stood at.

'It is an amazing and a thrilling site. But at a height,' Malcolm said calmly.

'Answer my question first,' Ian yelled.

'Turn on the GPS, Kathy,' Fred said. Kathy did as she was told. After a couple of minutes, Kathy said.

'It's showing the results.'

'Good. Where are we?' all of them asked together, at one time.

'It might be shocking.'

'Just tell,' Ian said.

'We are between the hills of the Girnar.'

Chapter 15

Two faces?

Everyone shot back in awe. Malcolm itched on his head. 'This is weird and confusing?' he said

'It really is. And the most confusing part of all is that we end up in the same place for which we had started,' Fred said.

'Actually we traveled 700km just for this? This is so ridiculous. Ending up in the same place you had started for and here you are, unaware of it,' Katie said with disgust.

'The map indirectly led us here,' Louis spoke after everyone had done their speaking. All eyes towards Louis now.

'And we've reached where we wanted to according to the map,' said Katie.

'Then why to wait. Let's just start our thing,' Malcolm said and he went back all the way to the point where the two exits confused them. All followed.

'Can anyone tell me what on earth are we?' Emma asked curiously while walking back to the point.

'We too don't know Emma. Be patient,' Fred said and they all reached where Malcolm was.

'All into the second exit, without any thinking,' Louis said, sounding pretty sure.

They all started walking inside the first tunnel. They had walked a good five yards of breathlessness and they reached a very huge metal room with nothing in it. All the sides of the room were covered with steel, silver in color, and visible due to a small white LED bulb hanging there. All the torches were powered on the wall right in front of them. The wall produced a ladder. They all advanced towards the ladder, taking care they wouldn't bump into something unusual. And in no time, they stood beneath the ladder. Malcolm asked for the torch from Katie and moved the torchlight in the path that the ladder went. After about three meters, the ladder ended with a trap door at its higher end. Moreover, it was unlocked.

'We've got to climb this ladder guys,' Malcolm said at last.

'Yes we will,' Emma said. 'Let's do it,' and she went up first. Louis, Katie, Ian, Fred, Malcolm and Kathy followed.

'What do I do now,' Emma shouted from the top.

'Push the trap door open,' Ian said from below. Emma with all her might pushed open the trap door. It opened surprisingly. This was an easy quest. Emma climbed in the trap door. One by one all of them climbed in. And there they were.

What they were in was a huge chamber with rocky walls and two LEDs with dimly blue lit lights above them. The chamber, more of a cave, was dark inside but everyone was delighted to have reached the zenith of their adventure, their aim, their game and their mission. The ten thousand disc shaped plates of gold lay right before them, glistening and lighting up the room. They were properly stacked for the auction, in rows and columns, one above the other, forming a gold wall. There were five rows one beside the other and four rows, each row containing five hundred gold discs.

'It's amazing,' Ian said, gaping at the marvelous sight.

'Never seen anything like this,' Louis spoke up.

Kathy, Katie and Emma had already started discussing about their girl fanatics just when Fred's sudden command shook them.

'We've got to transport these,' he said. 'As fast as we can. This is government property you see.'

'But how?' asked a tensed Malcolm.

'I've got an idea. On my search throughout the "M.Cryptic" I just found one thing that shocked me,' Fred said.

'And what would be that?' Ian questioned.

'It contained a trailer in it. And thus…' and Fred remained silent for a couple of minutes.

'I'm pretty sure we've got the rest of the part,' Emma winked to Fred.

Within the next hour, the discs were already being transferred. Malcolm pick up the discs which were placed high by standing on a ladder. He threw the disc to Ian then, who stood just beneath him, right beside the gold wall. Ian then passed the disc to Emma who stood near the trap door. Emma passed it on to Louis who stood at the foot of the ladder. Louis passed it to Katie who then passed it to Kathy and Fred. Kathy and Fred were the ones who were stacking the gold in a proper manner inside the truck. Yes, they had brought the trailer inside the tunnel. The tunnel was wide enough for that. And this chain continued for another two and half hours.

After the gold was all taken and stacked inside the trailer, Louis, Katie, Kathy and Fred waited for about twenty minutes for the other three to come down but in vain. Finally they decided to go and check in. When they ascended the ladder and got inside the trap door, they were shocked by what they saw. Emma, Ian and the brave Malcolm, all stood horrified looking in the direction where once the gold wall had been. And furthermore, what they saw next was the most unbelievable thing no one could have guessed of.

The place behind where the gold wall had been, there were three screens. A huge screen with two small ones beside it. Semi circular control panel lied below the screens. They could clearly see the silhouette of a man sitting on a chair, facing the screens.

'Welcome aboard, my friends. My dear, dear friends. My long lost friends and my one and only almost-going-to-die friend. Welcome to my abode. My second home,' the man sitting on the chair said, turning towards them, his face still hidden in the dark.

'Who is he?' Louis asked Malcolm.

'He is,' said Fred and shook everyone with a start, 'a lost friend turned foe and has an excellent record of friendship with us. A man with two faces and four tongues and takes revenge without anyone having anything done to him,' and he grinned.

'Ah! Well said dear Fred,' the man said in his cold insinuating voice. 'You've got all the possibilities to become an orator.'

'He knows are names too,' Katie whispered to Kathy, feeling terrible.

'Come on the point,' Malcolm said at last.

'How come you know our names?' Louis asked without fear.

'I don't need to come on the point. You have to come on my point and oh, you already are on my point,' the man said.

'Give yourself up,' Malcolm warned and in an instant, seven guns pointed themselves to the man.

'You want to kill me then. Try me. I'm not the only one here.'

'Who else do you have meat loaf?' Katie said.

'Your friend.'

'Which friend?'

And at the same time, Emma turned the gun, now ultimately pointing it towards Katie's head. She loaded the bullet. It was the clicking sound which gained everyone's attention. They all couldn't do anything but to look on.

'I told you I'm not alone,' the man said and burst out laughing. 'Over here Emma.'

Emma moved towards the man, still pointing the gun towards the others.

'He is the root of every hardship you all faced,' Emma said.

'And every adventure you came along,' the man said.

'One of your most trusted fellow.'

'The person who led you here.'

'One of the most brilliant brain.'

'And he is…'

The man came forward. A little light drew up on his face. A wry grin and the blue eyes decorated his face. He had a strong build. A blue shirt and black jeans covered him. 'Hey!' Katie yelled, 'that's Ian's shirt.'

'Well. This can't be Ian because Ian is with us,' Louis said.

'Ian never lets anyone touch his belongings.'

The man kept on advancing. After he was completely in front of them, Emma suddenly switched on the row of lights right above them, off white in color. Two strips of light ran on to meet the ends of the cave. Everyone except Fred and Malcolm stood in awe after looking at him, right below the light now.

'Mark!' they all exclaimed at once.

The man then started itching under his chin and pulled of the mask he wore.

Everyone was literally horrified; Fred and Malcolm included this time.

'Ian!'

Chapter 16

The Faithful Enemy

'I still don't get the confusion,' Fred said pretty casually. 'Ian is with us. Ian is there. Is Ian a ghost?' Louis questioned.

'Ian, tell us who is this? Your evil twin?' Katie asked the Ian with them.

'Actually, I'm not his evil twin. I'm Ian himself,' the man who had unmasked, said.

'Then who is the one with us?' everyone questioned in their minds.

'I'm sorry friends to betray you but,' the Ian with them said and he too itched under his chin and took of the mask. Everyo0ne was horrified to see the Ian with them. He wasn't Ian anymore. 'I'm Mark,' he said.

Everyone retreated. What on earth was happening? What was going on. Why had they put masks on their faces?

'So was it really you in everything,' Malcolm shouted at the top of his voice.

'Yes Malcolm. It was them from the very start,' Fred said calmly. 'Otherwise, why wouldn't I ask where is Mark? Now Ian.'

'That clearly mean you too knew about it Fred,' Kathy said. Fred nodded. 'Then why didn't you tell us?'

'You were not much concerned about Mark's rather Ian's disappearance, so I thought it would be better to reveal the mystery after we met our man and not ruin our mood.'

'Then what was the reason behind your doing this,' Louis said to the real Ian.

'He wanted to benefit himself by getting the gold with our help and then dumping us,' Malcolm popped in.

'Then that means everything by which we were going to be killed, he was the reason behind it.'

'Right.'

'Then if he wanted our help, why did he want to kill us before we could help,' Louis argued.

'Well. My main mission wasn't you. My main mission was finish you so that I could have all the gold to myself. I knew you'd anyhow reach here but I did keep everything ready but in vain. You finally reached here anyhow,' Ian said.

'Then where would you keep all the gold and transfer it?' Louis shot back in anger.

'Sorry to interrupt Ian,' Fred said, 'but the ship in which Malcolm and I came on this island, is Ian's own ship. The "M.Cryptic" stands for Mark Cryptic. And the trailer within it is also his. I came here in that very ship, killing all his acquaintances with a bazooka after making their way into the lifeboat and finishing them,' Fred said with the wide grin.

'That means the story which you told us, was about you?' Kathy asked, puzzled.

'Yes.'

'Enough of that,' said Mark. 'Wouldn't you all like to hear the next part.'

'Go ahead,' said Malcolm. 'I had doubts on you from the start. I was almost about to guess you two were behind it but my suspicions became final after Mark's disappearance on the ship and when I saw Ian, his build seemed not proper to me. I didn't know it was Mark in disguise. I concentrated on the eye color, surely not Ian's. Moreover, who would try to kill us preventing us from taking the gold unless it would not have been someone's selfishness. You're fools. All three of you. We caught you,' he yelled.

'But you can't do anything to us now,' Mark said pointing his gun towards Malcolm.

'And I have something more to say. You were silly too. I had a presentiment that if someone tried to kill us so many times, it is evident that he would keep a track upon us too. So your robotic bird camera did the trick. I shot it. Getting it guys?' Malcolm asked turning towards the others. Everyone nodded.

'And on top of that, Fred told me everything about these people, his deductions about the fake Ian and everything, while on the ship, coming to this island.'

'You did all this just for the sake of your adventure and benefiting yourself,' Katie spoke aloud, angrily.

'Yes,' Mark said, smiling. 'I and Ian were in contact from a long time, even before we all met at the "Indian Sultanate". We had all this planned very early. I then whispered into his ears to take up that topic. I knew you all would be interested and so, Ian spoke and you all agreed. That was great,' Mark said.

'You two timid fellows asked for your help because you knew you couldn't do this alone, right?' Kathy shot back.

'Who do you think then popped up the idea of the Kohinoor robbery? It was me. I wanted to test our eligibility as a team. And that is the reason I was hasty to rob it,' Ian said. 'And that is why I took up the danger.'

Everyone listened to him in awe.

'We mingled with your plans because we didn't want you to think we were outsiders. We were in a hurry to plan our further steps. I wanted to get here as fast as possible and execute everything before you came along, but my ship was delayed which I now learn was Fred's doing,' Ian said.

'And you failed. You ought to fail, all three of you,' Katie shouted in disgust.

'And one more thing. I put a bomb ion Kathy's house that night,' Ian said.

'It was you!' everyone exclaimed.

'Yes. I wanted to finish you all that time. You think you got the map under the Thames. You were wrong. I already had it from a long time, while I was in college,' Mark said. 'And I had placed it under the shattered fragments of the helicopter so that you would think you have an adventure. You have something to do which would indirectly lead us three to here and we succeeded.'

'Wait. When did Emma come into the picture then?' Malcolm asked.

'You have answered a good question Malcolm. Ian and me were in contact with Emma from a long time. Before we set off for Bombay, I phoned her and explained her everything. She came here and set up everything to make my work easier. My never broken contact with her helped us team up with her. And as for the helicopter which chased us that night after the Kohinoor robbery, it was Emma's. There was no plan about helping the Indian poor. It was just an excuse to reach here, with your help of course,' Mark said and smiled.

'You are a donkey Mark,' Katie yelled.

'Hang on. I'm not done yet. Fred, as he is alive, must have told you everything about his story of underwater. Well, I was the reason behind that too. It was my submarine, my plan, my man,' said Ian. 'I secretly jumped out of our ship with all my belongings. Another submarine already waited for me there. I went in that and reached here. Isn't it amazing?'

'I can no more hold my anger,' Malcolm said.

'It is very clear what had happened after that. I sent the planes but your bazookas ruined it,' Ian said.

'Now you know the reason I wasn't shooting them,' Mark said.

'I wasn't ready for that kind of event at all, but I had my backup plan ready.'

'And you have taken our map too, Ian,' Malcolm said. Ian's smile turned to a humorless expression.

'How do you know that?'

'We never went up again on the ship once we came down. And it was all muddy when I went there to take my Coke cans. So I know it was you,' Malcolm.

'I was cautious about you from the very start when I saw you whispering something in Ian's ears at the "Indian

Sultanate",' Fred said. 'You three acted very foolishly. And now,' he said walking up to Ian seated on the chair, 'you'll die. If anyone tries to do anything, including the girls, they die.'

Everyone knew how well built Fred was. No one dared to move.

Fred reached near Ian and all of a sudden punched him on the face.

Chapter 17

The Bullet On The Right

Ian's head turned towards one side. Fred whacked him a same one for the second time.

'Hold on,' Emma said pointing the gun to Fred. Fred grabbed the gun with relative ease and kept it in his pocket. Emma stood dumbstruck.

The next thing Fred did was punched him in the stomach now. Blood gushed forth from his mouth. The other six watched all this in horror. Fred punched and kicked him so much, his shirt was drenched in perspiration and Ian's shirt was drenched in blood.

'I had sent for the ship so that I could recover the gold on this island. But I didn't hear of it,' Ian kept on speaking, wiping the blood rushing down his clothes.

'How will you hear of it when every acquaintance of your is dead. There's no one on your side to pass you the information,' Fred said and punched him once more on the stomach.

'How did you finish them,' Ian now asked at last, his eyes flushing with anger.

'Well, I asked the man his leader's name. He said it was Ian. It all became clear to me. I lied to you guys. Sorry for that,' and saying this to the others, his whacked one more on Ian's nose.

'I then steered the ship here. Those foolish people of yours already had the map kept beside the wheel. I easily reached here,' Fred said. 'Bad luck,' Fred said and punched him on the face again. This time Ian blocked the attack. He twisted Fred's hand.

'You know who sent the shark underwater that day?' Ian yelled.

'It was you,' all answered in unison.

'You know who called the hydrosubs and why didn't Mark come upon our call of help underwater? It was me behind this,' he screamed. 'You pretty well now there are no sharks in the Thames.'

Suddenly with a reflex, Fred came out of his grasp and punched him on the biceps. Ian screamed sharply.

'You know how does a lion blast and a bird is set to fire, and the men who died in the helicopter that night were nowhere to be seen? It was all robots my friends. Robots made it all possible. In face the shark was also a robot. The fishes were robots. Everything was a robot to deceive you all. Isn't it amazing?' Ian said panting.

'I doubted it from the very start,' Louis said, clenching his teeth, with anger.

'But still you reached here but you shall not leave alive,' and Ian balled up his fist and hit Fred in the stomach. Ian fell. Fred swayed his hand to hit Ian randomly, but Ian blocked the attack and then powered two punches on Fred's face. Fred shattered.

'Anyone ready to try me,' Ian said, wiping the blood off his hands and then laughed wildly. No one replied for at least ten minutes.

Fred suddenly got up and hit Ian on the back of his head. Ian screamed loudly. It was a very powerful blow.

'Amazing isn't it?' Fred said and whacked him one more.

Ian screamed in agony. He couldn't bear the pain. He was bruised very badly.

'That is his weak point,' Malcolm said and went over, unafraid by the gun on his head and took the stick which Fred had and hit Ian on the head. One by one soon everyone except Mark and Emma came and hit a blow on Ian's head. Blood gushed out like a water fall.

'You'll die a very painful death Ian,' Fred said.

'Both, with your heart and body,' Kathy said.

'Within your own den,' Malcolm yelled.

'Right between us,' Louis said.

Ian wasn't in any condition to listen. He was in extreme pain.

'What you sow, so shall you reap,' Katie said after everyone had done their saying.

'Now see how betraying feels,' Malcolm said.

On the other side Emma stood, her body numb, not being able to move from the spot. Her eyes welled up with tears. She slowly and steadily pointed the gun in Ian's direction, standing on his left. Ian looked towards Emma. His eyes widened.

'Et tu Emma,' they said.

'I'm sorry,' Emma said.

The next moment a bullet hit Ian. Ian saw the left part of his body was clean. The bullet had been hit from his right. He made out the source of the bullet. It was Mark who had shot. With a final look at everyone, he departed from the world. Everyone's eyes were filled up with tears for some time. They sat there itself.

'May peace be with him,' Fred said, the last words uttered in the den.

Chapter 18

Back Again

'What an adventure,' Louis said as the gold filled truck was parked inside the ship again.

'Much of a mystery actually,' Katie said, correcting him.

All the seven of them including Emma stood there beside the "M.Cryptic", on the shores of the island.

'Ever wondered how you got between the hills of the Girnar though you traveled 700 km from Bombay?' Emma asked them.

'No,' everyone replied.

'The 700 km could be in any direction.'

'Right,' everyone said and smiled.

'Point,' Louis shouted after a while when he understood. Everyone chuckled.

After about two minutes of silence Emma said, 'Let's go aboard.'

Fred and Emma boarded the "M.Cryptic". the others boarded the "719". Malcolm stood on the shores with a grim, sad face. After about ten minutes, Fred called out.

'Hey! Want to come?'

Malcolm rushed up on the ship and thumped onto the beach chair on the deck itself.

'All set? Then let's go,' Fred said with excitement.

Both the ships blew their horns of victory and started simultaneously. They kept on going side by side. The early morning sun had colored the sky red and purple. The environment had changed. After about 70 km everyone came out of their ships with glasses and a variety of juices.

'Feeling great,' Louis shouted to Fred, while opening the orange juice bottle.

'Right. Have fun,' Fred replied and poured out three glasses of Coke and handed them over to his ship mates. Malcolm refused while Emma took it.

'Having fun?' Kathy shouted from the other ship.

'Our friend Malcolm, is refusing to enjoy?' Emma shouted.

'What has happened now?' Fred said going over to Malcolm and placing himself onto the beach chair beside Malcolm's.

'Two things are troubling me,' Malcolm said.

'And may I know those?'

'I was too hard on Ian. I mean I should not have taken that stick from you and...' and he cut off, his eyes welled up.

'Calm down Malcolm. Firstly it wasn't you the whole time. You were right in your own place. He got what he deserved. Don't worry about that. And what is the second thing?' Fred said pacifying Malcolm and sipping his juice.

'How did Emma help us?'

'When we found Emma, if you remember, I took her to my cabin and forced her to tell everything because it was the most unusual for a girl to be here without anyone and that no one knew about this island except us then how could she come on a holiday. She was lying. And then I made her tell everything. Moreover, we are best friends so fate played the rest of the game,' Fred said.

'He's right Malcolm,' Emma said. 'Cheer up now.'

'To cheer him up, offer him Coke,' Mark shouted. Fred gave the Coke glass to Malcolm. Malcolm accepted it this time.

'All right now?' Louis asked.

'He's cheered up,' Emma replied.

And the ships went on to reach Bombay.

Chapter 19

Gold

The friends reached Dublin again.

After three months, Fred barged inside Louis' apartment and showed the daily newspaper to Louis.

'See, I told you the story would be public.' Louis nodded.

'But how did it become public?' Louis asked.

'Well, I told everything to the newspaper company. I told our interesting story to them. They readily published the story of our honestly in the paper and here it is,' Fred said.

'Great thinking,' Louis said. 'I hope we do not fall into trouble.'

'No worrying. Have fun,' Fred said and left to show it to the others.

A lot of questions still remain unsolved. Louis thought and continued on his work.

Katie and Katie had joined the journalism field of work and were satisfied there.

Varun H. Parmar

Louis joined a robotic firm, a senior manager in it.

Emma was still studying the field of her choice.

Fred opted for orating and writing. And now he was on the way to be a great public speaker.

'Well Malcolm, I've one thing to ask you,' Mark said while walking down the street with Malcolm.

'And what may that be?'

'How did you know that the Spitfires were going to be there? They were meant to be concealed so well,' Mark said in anxiety.

'Well, I knew this question was going to come up so,' Malcolm said, opening his suitcase and taking out a newspaper, 'I kept this thing with me. It contains the news of a ship burst in flames by the planes, with the most economically powerful man on board. Lucifer Vicars.'

'Then how did you know it will come for you too?'

'Simple again,' and they stopped at the zebra crossing. 'You two didn't let even that man on the island. It was natural you would not let us too. So I came prepared.'

'I understand the confusion now,' Mark said, smiling a wry smile and they both parted for their destinations.

Mark went for automobiles and became a manager in a company.

Malcolm was the CEO of his own company and resumed his work.

"Thank God our lifestyles are still normal," everyone thought.

While all the friends were engrossed in themselves, Ian lay there, all alone on the "Au" island, between the hills of

132

the Girnar, in his own den, the bloody face intensifying horror, the eyes indicating that betrayal is the last thing you can do with mankind, covered in blood and lastly, below the ten thousand discs of gold.

A Note from the Author.

Please do read this my dear readers.

I know how much excited you are to know the mysteries which lie unrevealed. I promise you to unveil them soon enough in the next part of my book. My sincere apologies for not revealing them all.

I know the book has great twists and turns and there may be many parts which you would have not understood or the reason behind it. My apologies for that too.

And lastly, I would like to thank you for choosing my book and read it. Without your help, it would be practically impossible for me to have expressed my skill through the book.

(A fact. The book was started on 19th January 2013 and it contains exactly 19 chapters in it.)